Death Speaks Softly

by Anthea Fraser

DEATH SPEAKS SOFTLY
PRETTY MAIDS ALL IN A ROW
A SHROUD FOR DELILAH

Death Speaks Softly

ANTHEA FRASER

PUBLISHED FOR THE CRIME CLUB BY
DOUBLEDAY & COMPANY, INC.
GARDEN CITY, NEW YORK
1987

All of the characters in this book
are fictitious, and any resemblance
to actual persons, living or dead,
is purely coincidental.

Library of Congress Cataloging-in-Publication Data

Fraser, Anthea.
Death speaks softly.

I. Title.
PR6056.R286D4 1987 823'.914 86–32887
ISBN 0-385-24147-X

Printed in the United States of America
First Edition

Death Speaks Softly

CHAPTER 1

Bernard Warwick leant forward and peered at his face in the shaving mirror. It stared inscrutably back at him, and a smile twitched his mouth. "Shouldn't like to play you at poker, old man!" his colleagues would remark. "Never have the faintest idea what you're thinking!"

Which was as well, he reflected, lathering his face. (He preferred the traditional method of shaving, had not even unwrapped the electric razor his wife bought him years ago.) He'd learned young the necessity of hiding his feelings, and was not sufficiently interested in others to attempt to discern theirs. He accepted them at face value—they could afford him the same courtesy.

Face value. It was an effective mask, he acknowledged, studying in the glass the unlined brow from which dark hair was brushed uncompromisingly back. The cheeks had a healthy glow, and the clear, firm skin was that of a man half his age. Only the eyes, veiled with a wary blankness, might give an observer pause. It looked an unlived-in face, with no hint of the agony of living endured behind it. He was, in fact, fifty years old, which made it almost thirty since—

His hand trembled and a bright blood-bead stained the foam. Was it possible, he wondered, scraping the razor across his skin, to have a nervous breakdown without anyone being aware of it? What *was* a breakdown? A sense of isolation, searing despair? That had been his existence for the last thirty years. His one great terror was of cracking up. Sometimes he lay rigid in the night as Beryl slept beside him, imagining the disintegration of his personality, the crumbling to powder of brain, flesh, and sinew, all concealed behind that calm and placid façade.

How would they react, his university colleagues, were he led, gibbering, to a padded cell? With the cliché about genius and madness? He knew, without conceit, he was considered a genius. Knew, too, that such gifts as he possessed were the result of having flung all his repressions and frustrations into an academic career. "Professor Bernard Warwick of Broadshire University, the world's leading authority on the works of Brouge . . ." Yet, though they respected him, he'd no close friends. Beryl alone would weep for him.

Beryl! Why, in God's name, had he married her? In a last, panic-stricken attempt to forget the unforgettable? If he did have a breakdown, she'd have played her part in it, with her unending attempts to please him. Sometimes, in those agonising night watches, he considered murdering her. He would see himself, tall and unemotional in the dock, hear learned counsel ask, "But why, Professor Warwick? Why did you kill your wife?" And he would answer simply, "Because she loved me."

"Bernard?"

He jumped at the sound of her voice, as though it came from beyond the grave rather than the bathroom door.

"It's eight-fifteen, dear, and your breakfast's ready."

"Thank you. I shan't be a moment." He tipped some aftershave into his palm and patted it over his face. Enough of fantasy, the workaday world awaited him.

As, half an hour later, he backed his car out of the drive, his next-door neighbour emerged from his own house. Bernard raised a hand in salute. Tom Marshbanks was the closest he had to a friend, though the contact was maintained through their wives. The fleeting exchange cheered him. There were, after all, still some blessings he could count, and chief among them the town in which he lived. It never failed to please him and now, on a bright May morning, it was looking its best.

Steeple Bayliss, Broadshire's oldest settlement predating even Broadminster, was the seat of its university, and had, till the end of the last century, been its county town. Then, as new developments sprang up all over the county, its location tucked away in the north-west corner made administration less feasible, and it was superseded by the more central if less imposing Shillingham. The resentment and rivalry caused by this move had lasted to the present day, principally between the two football teams.

As Bernard made his way down the steep road into town, he revelled in the sunlit stone buildings tumbling towards the river and the magnificent viaduct by which he would shortly cross it. And as he did so, he glanced as he always did to his left, taking pleasure in the gently rocking boats at the quayside and the permanently moored *Barley Mow*, a large, converted barge which was now a public house and a favourite haunt of young people in the town. Even at this hour, tables were being set up on the quay alongside, and their gaily coloured umbrellas gave the scene a continental air.

Then he was across the river and following the road up towards the main gates of the campus. His academic day was about to begin.

That afternoon, in the house next to the Warwicks', Claire Marshbanks watched anxiously as her fifteen-month-old granddaughter lurched towards the bookcase.

"Had I better empty the shelves? Daddy's first editions aren't for chewing!"

"Don't fuss, Mum. She knows she mustn't touch them."

The child, inches from the bookcase, turned unsteadily and tapped the back of one hand with the other. "Ah-ah!" she said sternly.

The adults laughed. "What did I tell you?" Sarah said, triumphantly shaking back her hair. She looked ridiculously young to be a mother, Claire thought, but she was more confident with her firstborn than Claire herself had been.

"How's Paul? Still enjoying the new job?" Sarah's husband was deputy Head of Infants at the local primary school.

"He's loving it. Once Katy's old enough for playgroup, I'll apply for a part-time job there."

Claire made no comment. She'd be happier if Sarah waited till the child reached school age, but of course she was impatient to teach. She'd become pregnant within months of qualifying. "By the way, I asked Beryl to drop in. You don't mind, do you? I've a feeling time drags for her on the days she's not at Melbray, though she'd rather die than admit it."

"I don't mind, but she's heavy going, isn't she? She's so—intense, somehow, hanging on your every word. I just dry up."

Claire smiled. "Poor Beryl, she's so desperate to improve her I.Q., she drains every topic to its dregs. It's understandable, though. Being married to Bernard would give anyone an inferiority complex."

Katy sat down suddenly, absorbed in a glass ashtray she'd removed from the coffee table. Experimentally, she put it to her mouth.

"It's smooth, and perfectly clean," Claire said. "Edna washed all the ornaments this morning."

"Dear Edna, how is she? I haven't seen her for ages."

"The same as always. I was treated to a verbatim report of every conversation she's taken part in over the past week."

"Does she still call you 'Miss Claire' now you're a grandma?"

Claire laughed. "We knew each other as children, don't forget, with Ivy working for Granny."

"All the same, it sounds like something out of 'Dallas'!"

The telephone shrilled suddenly, and Claire leaned back in her chair to answer it. "Simon! Hello, darling. How are you?" She listened for a moment. "No, there haven't been any calls here. Why? . . . Perhaps she missed the train. What should I say if she does ring? . . . All right. Sarah's here, with Katy." She nodded at her daughter's mouthed message. "She sends her love . . . I will. Goodbye, darling. Take care."

"What's up with Sy?"

"He'd arranged to meet this French girl he knows, and she hasn't turned up."

"The *femme fatale* from the Uni?"

Claire looked surprised. "That's not how I'd describe her. I only met her briefly, but she seemed quite shy."

"From what I hear, half the campus is lusting after her. Is Sy smitten too?"

"I've no idea. He's taken her out a couple of times, but I think that's all."

"It might be enough!" Sarah said darkly. "What's she like?"

"Quite pretty, I thought, with a decidedly French air. Curly blond hair in a single plait, thick fair eyebrows and a small, pouting mouth." The doorbell rang. "There's Beryl now. Go and let her in, would you, darling. I'll keep an eye on the baby."

Beryl Warwick was small and thin. Her hair, a vibrant red in her youth, had faded to pepper-and-salt, and she had the pale skin usual with such colouring. Her face was pointed, her nose rather long, and she gave the impression of peering round it like an alert terrier on the scent of a rabbit.

She came quickly into the room, greeted Claire, and paused to coo at the baby. Katy, still intent on the ashtray, ignored her.

"Isn't she *growing,* Sarah? Before you know it, she'll be starting school! I've brought her some dolly mixtures. Is that all right?"

"How kind of you. Thank you. I'll take charge of them, shall I?"

Claire admired her tact, knowing that sweets were no part of Katy's diet. "I'll put the kettle on," she said.

Beryl perched on the edge of a chair, prepared to show interest in any comment Sarah might offer. Dutifully, the girl made an effort.

"Anything exciting coming up at Melbray?"

Melbray was a large manor house just outside town, now owned by a syndicate. It ran weekend leisure courses, antique shows, concerts, and conferences, and in the summer staged an ambitious outdoor theatre on the grounds. Claire and Beryl were on the organizing committee.

With the ball back in her court, Beryl spoke brightly. "Yes indeed. There's Art Appreciation next weekend. We've lined up some very good speakers, and it's fully booked. Then there's a week's residential course on French literature, and at the end of the month, a bank holiday pop concert." She made a little *moue.* "Not my taste, that one, but we cater for everybody and it will be carefully monitored. Entry by ticket only, and so on."

Claire returned with the tea tray and Sarah manoeuvred the baby into her own chair and tied a bib round her neck. Katy, anticipating food, began banging on the tray with the flat of her hands.

"May I help to feed her?" Beryl asked eagerly.

Sarah smiled. "She doesn't need help. She's an independent young lady, my daughter!"

Claire, noting the wistfulness on her friend's face, wished she'd primed Sarah beforehand. Beryl had married only ten years ago, at the age of thirty-eight, and the marriage was understandably childless. Claire found her silent worship of the baby touching.

"You haven't forgotten you're coming to dinner on Saturday?" she asked, handing Beryl her tea.

"No indeed, we're looking forward to it. It will do Bernard good to relax. At home, he always seems to have some work to do." Beryl's plain face lit up at the mention of her husband. She managed to introduce him into most conversations, as though to reassure herself of his existence. "Did I tell you he's been asked to do a paper on Brouge's early work? I know it's an honour, but he has so little time as it is. I'm afraid he'll burn himself out."

"Bernard takes everything in his stride," Claire remarked. "He'll pace himself; I'm sure you needn't worry."

"But I do," Beryl said simply. Then compressed her lips as though regretting the admission. If the late love which had come to her brought cares as well as joy, they were not for discussion over the tea table.

When tea was over, she stood up and replaced her cup and saucer on the tray. "Thank you, Claire, that was very pleasant. Lovely to see Sarah and Katy again." Her eyes lingered on the child's silky head. "Any time you want a babysitter, dear, you only have to ask."

Sarah looked up at her. "Really? You mean it?"

"Of course I do. I'm seldom out in the evenings. Bernard—" She broke off. "I can come any time. I'd enjoy it."

"Well, that's great. Having only just moved back here, we haven't sorted out babysitters yet. Thanks very much, I'll be in touch."

Beryl nodded and moved to the door. "Eight-thirty tomorrow, Claire?" They took turns in driving to Melbray.

"I'll be ready."

Claire saw her out, and Beryl walked the short distance to her own door. All the front gardens in the road were open-plan, but the Warwicks and Marshbanks shared a gravel walkway lying behind a grass island on the pavement, which was planted with multicoloured conifers. Claire's house was on the fringe of it, but the Warwicks' lay hidden from the road by graceful branches of fir and cedar. It was like being imprisoned in a wood, Beryl thought, seeing nothing but trees from her front windows.

She let herself into the house with a brief sigh, the bright eagerness which so daunted Sarah falling from her as she closed her front door. How lucky Claire was, she thought; a husband who adored her, a clever son and daughter, and now that darling grandchild. She clasped her hands tightly together. She wouldn't swap Bernard for anyone—of course she wouldn't—but if only he could be a *little* more demonstrative. Her whole purpose in life was to please him, to make his home comfortable, and to be a loving, intelligent wife; but he gave no sign of noticing her efforts. Perhaps he took them for granted—and perhaps, she excused him loyally, it was right that he should.

Occasionally, shyly, she'd force the issue. "Do you like my new dress, Bernard?" Or, "Did you enjoy the chicken? It's a new recipe." No hint that she'd spent the entire day marinating, stuffing, and basting. But whatever the question, his reply never varied. "Yes, dear, it's very nice."

Sometimes, yearning for confirmation of his love, she'd touch his hand, yet though he'd smile and pat her arm, she felt unaccountably that she'd embarrassed him. But then Bernard wasn't like other men, and she shouldn't expect him to be. He was brilliant—everyone said so. He could have had anyone he wanted—and he had chosen her. The wonder of it still amazed her. So—what was she worrying about? She gave herself a little shake and, as she walked briskly through to the kitchen, was already planning the evening meal.

Late that night, a man lay staring into the darkness, oblivious of his wife sleeping beside him. Silly little bitch—what did she think she was playing at? It wasn't as if he'd taken her by surprise. He'd made it pretty clear what he wanted.

And she hadn't objected to his kisses, he thought, pulses racing at the memory of rounded limbs and fluttering eyes. But when she'd really got him going, when he could hardly contain himself, she'd just pulled away, glanced at her watch, and announced that she had a train to catch! A *train!* He'd thought she was joking, had laughed and buried his mouth in her neck. But she began struggling, pushing at his hands, and he'd felt the accelerated beat of her heart.

"Please no, monsieur!" (Monsieur! Made him sound about ninety!) "I assure you, it is true. I have an appointment, in Shillingham."

"Then he'll have to wait, won't he, till we've finished here."

"But you don't understand! I must demand that you return me to town."

"Demand?" He'd stared at her, aware even then that the imperious word had been only a slip in translation.

"Beg," she amended swiftly. "*Je vous implore, monsieur. On m'attend.*"

No wonder he'd lost his temper. All that startled innocence all of a sudden. Who was she kidding? Everyone knew about French girls.

God, he'd been a fool to get involved with her! But she was so luscious, so golden, like a ripe peach he longed to sink his teeth into. He groaned softly in the darkness, turning his head from side to side till his wife stirred in her sleep.

Well, he'd taught her a lesson, anyway. And serve her right, playing fast and loose like that. There were names for girls like her. But he wished to God it hadn't happened, that he could turn the clock back. That was one mistake he'd never make again. The only consolation was that neither would she.

Philip Baker stormed into the tutors' common room and flung his briefcase on the table.

"Yet again that bloody French girl hasn't showed up. Talk about unreliable! She didn't phone in, did she?"

Mark Lennard looked up from his papers. "Not that I've heard."

"It's the second time in ten days, for God's sake. Last week it was something to do with her liver."

Mark laughed. "The French are obsessed with their livers. Surely you know that?"

"What I do know is there's no one available at such short notice to take her class. She seems to think she can come and go as she pleases."

"Calm down, Phil! What about a spot of *entente cordiale?* The girl's probably ill."

"Then I'd feel a damn sight more *cordiale* if she'd inform me of the fact."

It wasn't until Arlette Picard failed to return to her lodgings on Wednesday evening that anyone registered more than annoyance at her absence.

"I wonder what's keeping her?" Mrs. King said worriedly, gazing out of the window. "She's always back by this time—she knows we eat at seven."

"She thinks it's too early—she told me," her daughter volunteered.

"Well, I'm sorry about that, but I'm not going to change the habits of a lifetime to suit her ladyship. When at Rome, do as Rome does." She glanced again at her watch. "You'd think she'd phone if she was going to be this late. She's usually good about that."

"Why not ring the university? She might still be in the library."

"Not this late, surely."

Iris shrugged, returning to her magazine, and after a minute her mother went to the phone. But when she succeeded in locating someone from the French Department, the news was not reassuring.

"Iris, she hasn't been in today!"

"That's odd." Iris frowned. "How did she leave it yesterday?"

"She said she'd a date in Shillingham that afternoon, and as she hadn't a class till mid-morning, she'd probably spend the night there."

"With Sophie, I suppose. That's where she stayed a fortnight ago."

"That's what I thought. So I didn't expect her last night, and I supposed she'd go straight to work this morning. But if she never turned up—" Mrs. King turned, staring at her daughter. "Sophie's an au pair, isn't she? Do you know the name of the family?"

"No." Iris stared back at her. "God, I hope she's all right."

"Who was she meeting in Shillingham, have you any idea?"

"Simon Marshbanks, I should think."

"Give him a ring, love. He may know something."

But Simon wasn't in, and his flat mate didn't know when he'd be back.

"I shouldn't worry, Mum," Iris said bracingly. "He's probably with her now. If they'd arranged to meet tonight too, she might have stayed on and skipped the class. I wouldn't put it past her."

"Perhaps you're right. Well, I'm not going to hold supper any longer. I'll leave Arlette's in the oven."

Nevertheless, they spent an uneasy evening, their ears tuned for the sound of the front door. But it never came. When Mrs. King went to the kitchen last thing to let the cat out, she found the oven still on. She took out the plate, stared blankly at the dried-up food on it, and tipped it into the bin. Then she gave a superstitious little shudder. If there was no word from Arlette by the morning, she'd have to contact the police.

CHAPTER 2

Detective Chief Inspector David Webb stood in his office staring moodily out of the window. Below him, the gravel driveway shimmered in the sunlight, and the lawn with its fishpond in the centre lay smooth as brushed velvet. Beyond the gateway, on Carrington Street, women shoppers in gaily coloured dresses hurried past. Out there in the sunshine everyone seemed happy and full of purpose. He sighed deeply.

"What is it, Dave?" Alan Crombie inquired from behind him. "You've an aura like a thundercloud this morning."

"Sorry, I'm just thoroughly browned off."

"On a gorgeous day like this?"

"Particularly on a gorgeous day like this. Half the trouble is having nothing interesting to do. We've not had a case to get our teeth into for weeks, and I'm up to here with paperwork."

Half the trouble, he had said. And the other half was Hannah. More specifically, having caught sight of her yesterday evening, going into the Grand Theatre on the arm of some dark, self-satisfied-looking bastard. Furthermore, it was the second time in just over two weeks he'd seen her in the same company. No wonder the bloke looked pleased with himself.

God, he must have been mad, losing his cool that way over Susie. Having been married to her for eleven years, he should have known there was no chance in hell of their coming back together. Instead of which, he'd allowed the old chemistry to flare up again, and all three of them had been hurt. He and Susan had at least gone into it with their eyes open, but how could Hannah be expected to understand?

And that was nearly eight months ago. Eight months of

putting off contacting her, telling himself that, living in the same building, they'd be sure to bump into each other. But Hannah had taken care that they shouldn't, and who could blame her? So why should he be surprised, now, to see her with someone else?

There was a tap on the door. He ignored it, and after a moment Alan called, "Come in."

"Excuse me, sir—" Young Marshbanks, by the sound of it.

"Yes?" He went on staring out of the window.

"Could I have a word?"

With a sigh, Webb turned. The detective constable looked across at him apologetically, his usually cheerful face subdued.

"All right, Simon. What is it?"

Alan Crombie pushed back his chair, murmured something about checking records, and left the room.

"Well, sir, I don't want to speak out of turn, and strictly speaking this isn't our business—"

"Suppose you start at the beginning?" Webb suggested heavily.

"Yes, sir. Well, there's a French girl I know, sir, and she's very interested in horses." Marshbanks flushed, noting his superior's raised eyebrow. "She's been on at me for weeks to show her round the stables, so I fixed it with the station sergeant for Tuesday afternoon. And she never turned up."

"Simon," Webb began warningly, "if you're proposing to enlist me to sort out your love-life—"

"No, sir, really. The point is, she should have arrived on the two-thirty from Steeple Bayliss, but she didn't, and no one's seen her since. Her landlady's daughter's just been on, asking if I know where she is."

"I hope you advised her to get in touch with their local station?"

"Yes, sir, but—well, there are one or two things we could do more easily at this end. I don't want to butt in on their territory, but—"

"And exactly what could we do better at this end?"

"She told her landlady she might stay Tuesday night with a friend in Shillingham, an au pair. But they don't know the name of the family. All Iris could tell me was that they live near the golf club and have a little boy called Ben. I thought perhaps if we contacted the playgroups or primary schools in the Lethbridge Road area—"

"Is this an official inquiry?" Webb interrupted.

"No, sir. Not yet."

Webb sighed. "Then you know as well as I do that our hands are tied. What's this French girl of yours doing over here, anyway?"

"She's at the university, sir, working for her Ph.D. But she also takes conversation classes, and does a bit of coaching."

"Well, leave it with me." He looked at his watch. "It's twelve-twenty now. I'll phone SB after lunch and see if they could use a bit of help. That satisfy you?"

"Yes, sir. Thank you, sir."

Lunch in The Brown Bear raised Webb's spirits marginally, and, noting Marshbanks' carefully bent head as he returned to his office, he decided to give Chris Ledbetter a buzz as promised. Anything to postpone a return to the paperwork.

"Dave! Talk about coincidence! Were your ears burning?"

"No, why?"

"I was just wondering if I could justify getting in touch with you. I don't know if you heard, but I broke my ankle a couple of weeks back." He brushed aside Webb's expressions of concern. "Oh, I can hobble to work—just. Happy calls for me and drives me home afterwards, but once here, I'm pretty well desk-bound, which is bloody frustrating, as you can imagine."

"And where do I come in?"

"Well, a case has just cropped up and I'm not sure I like the smell of it. Girl seems to have vanished—and a French girl, at that."

"Well, well!" Webb commented. "You're right about coincidence. That's why I was ringing you." He explained about Marshbanks' concern.

"Yes, that's the one, all right. I've had my lads out this morning making routine inquiries, but no one's falling over themselves to co-operate. Look, have you a lot on at the moment?"

"Damn all. I'd be glad of something to do. I'll clear it with the Super and be right over."

"Fine. But Dave, before you come, have another word with that lad of yours. Anything at all on this girl could be crucial."

Simon Marshbanks sat across the desk from Webb, Sergeant Jackson at his side.

"It seems," the DCI was saying, "that SB are taking this seriously, and they'd like us to give them a hand. So tell me everything you can about this girl, Simon. Damn it, I don't even know her name."

"Arlette Picard, sir."

"Description?"

"Quite tall—five-six or seven. Fair hair, sometimes in a plait and sometimes loose. Blue eyes. Weight about eight and a half stone."

"Age?"

"Twenty-four, I think she said. She's been through a French university—it's a doctorate she's working on here."

"And how did you meet her?"

"Through a friend of mine, Peter Campbell. She's in digs next door to him."

"Landlady's name and address?"

"Mrs. King, 24, Farthing Lane."

"Do you know the girl's home address?"

"No, but she comes from Angers."

"Spell it."

Marshbanks did so. He'd pronounced it "Onjay." That's what came of going to a posh school, Webb reflected philosophically. Young Simon's scholastic connections had been of help to them in the past. "How well do you know her? Intimately?"

Simon's habitually red cheeks flamed, and beside him, Jackson moved uncomfortably. "No, sir. Nothing like that."

"Sorry," Webb said briefly, "but we need to get the facts straight."

"We went to one or two of the same parties and got on quite well. For some reason she's intrigued by my being in the police—she calls me '*Flic.*' But I've only taken her out twice, once to the cinema and once for a drink. We'd planned to spend the rest of Tuesday together and have a meal at the Hong Kong. She's mad on Chinese food."

"Has she any regular boyfriends—anyone who might be jealous?"

"No one serious. She goes round with a crowd."

"Any names you can remember?"

"Afraid not." He grinned, looking suddenly very young. "If anyone's jealous, it's probably the girls. Arlette's the star attraction at the moment, and I can see why. She's so different."

"And accommodating?"

"I don't think so, sir. She enjoys flirting, but I'm pretty sure that's as far as it goes. In some ways she's a very private girl."

"All right, Simon, that's all for now. Get hold of John Manning and see what you can suss out in the Lethbridge Road area. If you come up with anything, contact us at SB."

As they walked round to the carpark, Jackson said diffidently, "You reckon we'll be taking this case on, guv?"

"It looks like it, Ken, with DI Ledbetter semi-laid up."

"Hope it doesn't drag on too long."

Webb glanced at him in surprise, then understanding came. Jackson's wife was expecting twins, and they were due any day. "SB's only a fifty-minute drive, Ken. Leave Millie their number, if it'll make you feel happier."

Jackson grinned shamefacedly. "I already have."

"Your mother-in-law's arrived, hasn't she? Well then, there's nothing to worry about."

There spoke a childless man, Jackson reflected, starting up the car.

It was a lovely day for a drive, and Webb leaned back in his seat, determined to enjoy it. He wished the French girl no harm, but he was grateful to have something to occupy his mind other than Hannah and her new escort.

"Interesting place, Steeple Bayliss," he remarked, to distract his sergeant from domestic worries. "Know it at all?"

"I've been over a couple of times."

"That chasm it's built on was carved out by the last ice age. The town grew up on the north side, which has the more gradual slope, but the south bank was uncultivated right up to the nineteenth century, when the university was built there."

"Fancy!" said Jackson absently.

Webb laughed. "OK, I'll spare you the potted history. I read the guide book once, and bits of useless information stuck."

Jackson grinned. "All I really know about SB I got from Bob Dawson."

"Don't tell me—the iniquities of its football team!"

Their journey took them through the small market town of Marlton. In this north-west corner of Broadshire, its proximity to the Cotswolds was apparent in the honey-coloured stone buildings and the increasingly hilly countryside.

"I'd forgotten how lovely it is up here," Webb commented, looking about him with an artist's delight. "My next free day, I'll come along with my sketch pad."

The Marlton road brought them into Steeple Bayliss at the far end of its High Street. They crawled along it for a mile or so behind a line of buses, private cars, and lorries, until with relief they turned down a side street leading to the lower level of Maybury Street and the local police station.

Chris Ledbetter awaited them in his office, his injured ankle propped on a stool beneath his desk. "Excuse me not getting up, Chief Inspector," he said formally, for the benefit of the two sergeants. "I think you've met Sergeant Hopkins. He's my right arm—or rather foot—at the moment."

The sergeant was a tall, thin man with a long and lugubrious face. He nodded at them gloomily, and Webb repressed a smile. He remembered "Happy" Hopkins from his last visit. He introduced Jackson, and they were asked to sit down.

Inspector Ledbetter was almost indecently goodlooking. His thick blond hair had the faintest suggestion of a wave, his gentian blue eyes were set under straight brows, his shoulders were broad, and his waist narrow. Furthermore his smile, as Webb had noted more than once, could be devastating. Men tended to underrate him, women—even the most respectable—found themselves fluttering their eyelashes. Yet he was happily married to a nice woman you wouldn't look twice at, and had a teenage daughter of whom he was inordinately proud.

"The position so far is this," he was saying. "The last authenticated sight of the girl was when she left her lodgings on Tuesday morning. She was wearing an outfit she'd bought only the previous day—camel-coloured linen skirt, pale blue top, fuchsia kerchief round her neck. High-heeled sandals, bare legs. She told Mrs. King she'd an afternoon date in Shillingham—presumably with your lad, Chief Inspector—but didn't say what she was doing that morning. Which, we think, is the crux. Because as far as we can make out, she never left here. By all accounts she's a pretty girl, specially when she wears her hair loose as she did that day. There was an impressionable lad on the ticket barrier on Tuesday, and there's no way she'd have passed him without his noticing her."

"Buses?" Webb inquired.

"As you know, they take longer, but we've made inquiries at the depot and no one remembers her there either. Leaving private cars, which we're working on now."

"Marshbanks expected her by train—he went to meet the

two-thirty. That would be—what—about one-fifty from here?"

"One forty-eight, yes. So there you have it. We've no trace of her after she left Farthing Lane at ten-ten that morning."

"So if she was intending to catch the train and didn't, the time we're looking at is between ten-ten and one forty-eight."

"It would seem so, yes. Three hours and forty minutes. A lot can happen in that time. Has your DC any names that might help?"

"No, but she seems to have quite a few friends, presumably from the university. We'll have to start tracking them down. In the meantime, Marshbanks is trying to discover where she meant to spend Tuesday night, though if you reckon she never reached Shillingham, that mightn't be much help."

A tap on the door heralded a girl with a tea tray and four cups, which she distributed with a smile.

"We've a house to house underway," Ledbetter continued as she went out. "With foreign nationals you can't be too careful. She *might* have taken it into her head to go home, but it seems unlikely. We checked ports and airports without any joy." He paused, and added expressionlessly, "And we're dragging the Darrant."

Jackson repressed a shudder. He'd rowed the family down the river on his last visit, and he thought of the pretty, bobbing boats, and the pub that was an old barge. Was that idyllic scene to be the backdrop to tragedy? As a father himself—and shortly to be one again—he felt a wave of sympathy for the anxious French parents, which intensified as Ledbetter added, "In the circumstances, I thought her parents should be informed. We've asked the French police to contact them."

The phone rang. Ledbetter lifted it, listened for a moment, and handed it to Webb. Marshbanks' voice came over the wire.

"We've located the au pair's family, sir. Mr. and Mrs. Willoughby, of Lethbridge Close. Arlette spent the weekend there a fortnight ago, to keep Sophie company while they were away; but they haven't seen her since. Sophie says Arlette asked last week if she could stay Tuesday night, but nothing definite was fixed, and when she didn't turn up, Sophie thought she'd changed her mind."

"How well does this Sophie know Arlette?" Webb asked.

"They met a few months ago in a department store. Arlette heard her struggling to find the right words, and helped her out. They've met several times since."

"Has she any names which might help us?"

"One or two, sir, mainly from the campus. Shall I read them out?"

"No, they'll keep till I get back. We'll leave the university till tomorrow; they'll be finishing for the day by now. Put a list on my desk, with any relevant comments. And well done, Simon. Your hunch paid off."

He replaced the phone and repeated the findings to an attentive audience. "He feels responsible," he ended quietly. "He's thinking that if he'd made some positive move to look for her instead of taking the huff, she might have turned up by now." He looked at Ledbetter. "Who did you speak to at the university?"

"Professor Warwick, head of the French Department. He says he didn't know the girl well." He turned to his sergeant. "Take Sergeant Jackson to the main office, Happy, and introduce him to the lads—we'll be working together on this one."

Happy nodded morosely and motioned Jackson out with a jerk of his head. As the door closed behind them, Ledbetter smiled.

"Happy's mortified that extra help has been called in. To be fair, he's taken on the hell of a lot since my accident, and managed extremely well. He feels quite capable of seeing the inquiry through."

"And it's an added insult that we're from Shillingham?" Webb suggested with a smile.

"Got it in one. But missing persons are tricky. You have to pull the stops out, even though you half expect them to turn up any minute and ask what all the fuss is about."

Webb nodded. "But it's no use telling a distracted parent eighty-five percent turn up of their own accord."

"As luck would have it, this is our second case in two weeks. Young girl disappeared after a row with her mother. For my money she's skipped to London and is lying low for a while, but we've a full-scale search underway. That's my problem, but it does mean we're already at full stretch, which was another reason for contacting you. I'm just sorry you'll have so much travelling. If it would help, we've a spare room you'd be more than welcome to, and we could soon fix your sergeant up."

"Good of you, Chris, but no thanks. I'll have to look in at DHQ every day, and Jackson's wife's expecting any minute. He'll be anxious to get home at night."

"Well, at least you must have a meal with us while you're over. Janet will be pleased to see you, and you'll notice a big change in Emma. She's quite a young lady now."

"That'd be great." Webb stood up and stretched. "I reckon there's not much else we can do at the moment. I'll go and read the Willoughbys' statement and see what names Marshbanks has come up with. And I'll be here by eleven in the morning."

The phone rang again. Chris Ledbetter listened, spoke into it, and nodded, his face grim. As he replaced it, he met Webb's eye. "The French parents are arriving tomorrow. Flying to Heathrow and getting the train up here, due at three-fifteen. The university's sending someone to meet them, but we should also put in an appearance."

"OK, Chris, I'll stand in for you, but I hope their bloke speaks French."

"You might think, Ken," Webb said in the car back to Shillingham, "that DI Ledbetter should be modelling knitwear, but don't underestimate him. It's a mistake a lot of people make."

The sergeant, with his thinning, sandy hair, grinned. "I wish I had his problems!"

"They're real enough. People aren't inclined to take him seriously with looks like that, so he has to work twice as hard to win them round. But he's a great bloke and a first-class police officer."

Jackson was thinking of his words as he turned into his driveway and garaged the car. The sound of children's voices came from the back garden, and his spirits rose as they always did. Wherever he'd spent the day and whatever he'd been doing, Ken Jackson loved coming home. With his door key in his hand, knowing Millie and the kids awaited him, he wouldn't change places with anyone—even DI Ledbetter, he thought with a grin.

As the garage door clanged down, Paul and Vicky erupted through the side gate, hurling themselves against him, and shouting above each other to impart their news of the day. The commotion brought their grandmother out of the house.

"That's quite enough, you two. Quieten down and let your father draw breath. In you come, Ken, the kettle's just boiled."

"How's Millie?" he asked, following her into the house.

"No change. I think she'll be glad, now, when it's over. Go in and see her while I pour your tea. And you children, back into the garden till I give you a call."

Jackson smiled at her, grateful for the kindly control she exercised over his children while their mother was laid up. He'd never understood the traditional dislike men had for their mothers-in-law. Mrs. Banks, rounded and motherly, with her fair hair fading almost unnoticeably into grey, looked as he imagined Millie in thirty years' time, and he loved her accordingly.

He opened the living-room door quietly, in case Millie was asleep. She was on the sofa with her feet up, but she turned with a smile and held out her hand. He came quickly to take it, bending to kiss her.

"OK, love?"

"OK, yes. How about you? What kind of a day have you had?"

He drew up a chair and sat beside her. "Well, as you know we went haring off to Steeple Bayliss. Some French kid's gone missing, and everyone's running round in circles." He grinned, knowing she loved to hear the details of his day. "You should have seen the DI over there. Wow! Robert Redford has nothing on him!"

Millie laughed. "Really? Tell me more."

"Mr. Webb reckons he's a good egg, but he looks like a film star—yellow hair, purple eyes, flashing smile."

"And he can't find his missing persons without you?"

"Well, he's broke his ankle, see, and can't get out of the office."

His mother-in-law came into the room, and Jackson brought a table across for her to set down the tray. Beyond the French windows he could see the kids. Paul was halfway up an apple tree, Vicky dancing about beneath it. Please God the next two would be as healthy. It had been a shock when Millie's pregnancy was diagnosed as twins. Still, she was a born mother, bless her, and now Vicky was at school things shouldn't be too hectic.

"Did you see the doctor today?" he asked.

"No, I'm going tomorrow, to have my blood pressure checked. If it's still up, I might have to go in early."

"Well, everything's under control here," her mother said comfortingly. "You've nothing to worry about, has she, Ken?"

"Not a thing. All you have to do is produce the nippers and take things easy."

Millie said casually, "Going back to SB tomorrow?"

"Might." Jackson was equally offhand, knowing full well he would be. "Still, you've got the number, love, and I can be back within an hour if you want me."

"Yes, of course." Smiling determinedly, Millie accepted her cup of tea.

At about the same time, Beryl Warwick popped round next door. Claire, who had parted from her only half an hour earlier on their return from Melbray, was surprised to see her.

"Have you heard the news?" Beryl began excitedly before she was even inside the house. "The police have been up at the university all day. Apparently some French girl's disappeared, and they're interviewing everyone who knows her."

Claire stared at her, her eyes widening in distress. "Not Arlette, surely?"

The interruption stopped Beryl in mid-flow. "Yes, that's the name. Do you know her?"

"But, Beryl, are you sure? There can't be some mistake?"

"No, Arlette Picard. Bernard's just been telling me about it."

"But she's a friend of Simon's!" Claire said helplessly.

"Really?" Beryl's long nose quivered with excitement. "He must know about it, I suppose?"

"I don't know. He phoned on Tuesday, just before you came, to ask if she'd been in touch. He was expecting to meet her in Shillingham and she hadn't arrived."

"And she's not been seen since!" Beryl reported with relish.

"I'll phone Simon." Claire turned distractedly into the sitting-room and Beryl followed her, waiting eagerly as Claire dialled. "Oh, darling, you are back. Thank goodness! Beryl is here, with a most disturbing story about Arlette. Do you know anything?" She listened, her face grave. "But, Simon, that's dreadful! Do you think something's happened to her? . . . Yes, I see . . . Oh, poor souls. How terrible for them. Well, do keep me in touch. Having met her, I shall be worrying."

"Well?" Beryl inquired. "Who are the poor souls?"

"The girl's parents—they're coming over. What on earth can have happened to her, Beryl?"

"Search me. I knew about the parents; Bernard's meeting their train. They've been booked in at The White Swan."

"Imagine how they must be feeling."

"Yes." Beryl hesitated, but having imparted her bombshell, she'd nothing else to offer. "Well, I must get back. I left the potatoes on, but I thought you'd like to know. Not that I realized you'd met the girl, or that she's Simon's girlfriend."

"But she isn't," Claire contradicted automatically. "He doesn't know her well."

Only after Beryl had gone did she analyse that response, and was frightened by its implications. If, God forbid, something *had* happened to Arlette, any boyfriends would be the first to be questioned. But Simon was in the *police*, for heaven's sake! Surely that made a difference. *Was* he really fond of her, as Sarah wondered? Quite suddenly, in her sunlit sitting-room and for the first time in her life, Claire Marshbanks felt under threat. It was with overwhelming relief that she heard her husband's key in the door.

CHAPTER 3

By ten-fifteen the next morning, Webb and Jackson were back in Steeple Bayliss with the list of names Sophie'd given Marshbanks. For the most part they were Christian names only—Steve, Mike, Charlie, and so on. Two others were more promising—Dr. Lightbody and Mr. Duncan—but Sophie was uncertain whether Arlette had spoken of them in the context of work or leisure.

They stopped first at the police station, where Webb handed over the list. "Perhaps your men could start on the unattached names, Chris; they may take some tracking down. I'll call on Lightbody and Duncan, along with Professor Warwick, but I want to see the landlady first. Could I borrow a street map?"

Ledbetter produced one from his desk. "Farthing Lane's just above the High Street and parallel with it. Ten minutes' walk. I'd advise leaving the car here till you go to the university; parking can be tricky in the town centre."

On arrival at Farthing Lane, Webb found only Mrs. King at home. Her daughter Iris was at the library, where she worked. "Go and have a word with her, Ken," Webb instructed. "I'll join you in a few minutes. Miss Picard might confide in someone her own age."

"Yes, she and Iris do chat sometimes," Mrs. King agreed. Her eyes filled with tears. "Oh dear, Chief Inspector, I hope she's all right."

"So do we, Mrs. King." He nodded to Jackson, and followed the woman into the front room. Its decor would have been ultra modern in the sixties—stark white walls and blue woodwork. Uncomfortable-looking chairs were positioned on the carpet, and a carved animal of unknown species stood in the centre of the mantelpiece.

"Now, just a few details, Mrs. King, to put me in the picture." Webb spoke easily, to help her relax. "How long has Miss Picard been with you?"

"Since October, when she came to the university. She's a nice girl, no trouble at all." Led by Webb, she repeated her account of her last sight of Arlette. "I thought how fresh and pretty she looked. She'd bought the skirt and top the day before, from Next, and the colouring really suited her."

Arlette had dressed in her best clothes. For Simon Marshbanks, or for someone else, earlier?

"You say you expected her to be away overnight. Did she take her toothbrush and night things?"

Mrs. King put a hand to her mouth. "Do you know, I never thought to look." She excused herself and hurried from the room.

"You're right, Chief Inspector, she did!" she exclaimed on her return. "Fancy me not thinking of that!"

"She took a suitcase, then?"

"No, just the large shoulder-bag she usually wore."

"What about her passport?"

"I saw it just now, when I checked in her drawer. All her other things are still there."

So although an overnight stay at Shillingham had been in mind, Arlette hadn't contemplated a longer absence. "Do you know if she'd any contacts outside the university?"

"She did some private coaching, in French."

Webb took out his notebook. "Where?"

"The Morgans in Tewkesbury Close on Mondays, and the Palfry twins on Thursdays. They live in Westfield Road."

Webb noted it down. "Anyone else she saw?"

"She's been out a couple of times with the Campbell boy next door, and Simon Marshbanks too, I think." She paused. "But you'll know about that."

Her tone held a veiled question, but Webb ignored it. "Did she talk about them at all?"

"Not really. She did say, 'Imagine! Little Simon a *flic!* It's *bizarre!*' That's a favourite word of hers."

Little Simon. Had she meant in height or years? Marshbanks was stocky, and though not really short, might appear so to a tall girl in high heels. As to his youth, his fresh complexion made him look younger than he was.

"Has she had any problems that you know of?" Mrs. King shook her head. "And her health's good?"

"She did have an upset last week. Stayed in for two days. Her liver, she said it was, but it seemed like a bilious attack to me."

"Nothing serious, though?"

"Oh no."

"What does she do in her spare time? Has she any hobbies?"

"She's horse-mad. Goes to the stables in Wagon Lane two or three times a week. And she plays tennis sometimes, with Peter Campbell."

Though he stayed a few more minutes, Mrs. King had little else to contribute. The interview over, Webb set out for the Library to rejoin Jackson, hoping he might have done better with the daughter. And it was as he turned the corner on to the High Street that he came face to face with Hannah. His own shock was mirrored on her face, but there was no polite way she could avoid him—and Hannah was always polite.

"Hannah!" He caught her arm in a subconscious attempt to detain her. "What on earth are you doing here?"

"Hello, David." Her breathing was uneven, but her grey eyes held his as steadily as ever. "I might ask you the same."

"Official business. A girl missing from the university."

"I've been up there, too. I brought three of the Lower Sixth to look round before filling in their UCCA forms."

"Have you time for a coffee?"

"Oh, I'm afraid I—"

"There's a café just along here." He propelled her firmly down the pavement, giving her no chance of further protest.

His mind was in a turmoil, planning and instantly discarding what he could say to her. It wasn't until they were seated that he remembered Jackson waiting at the library. Well he'd just have to kick his heels for another ten minutes; this unlooked-for opportunity couldn't be lost.

She looked lovely, he thought, slim and immaculate in a grey linen suit, her tawny hair shining. He smiled at her, but she didn't respond; merely met his eyes gravely, and waited.

"It's been a long time," he said quietly.

"Yes." She wasn't going to help him.

"You'd think that, living in the same building, we'd bump into each other."

She didn't reply, confirming his conclusion that she had taken evasive action. The waitress brought the coffee he'd ordered, and he waited till she moved away. Then he said gently, "How have you been, Hannah?"

"Fine." There was a defiant ring to the word.

He started to speak but, perhaps fearing he was going to broach personal subjects, she forestalled him. "Tell me about the missing girl. When did she disappear?"

So be it. In any event, The Rest Awhile was hardly the place for intimate discussion. So he told her about Arlette and that he was due to meet her parents that afternoon.

"That will be difficult. I hope you have some good news by then."

"Good news is in short supply at the moment." He swallowed the coffee quickly, feeling it scorch his tongue. "I must go, Sergeant Jackson's waiting for me." He signalled the waitress, paid the bill, and got to his feet.

"Thanks for the coffee," she said.

"A pleasure. It's—good to see you again." He walked quickly across the room and pushed his way through the door. Had he looked back, he'd have seen that her eyes, following him, were full of tears.

Jackson was pacing up and down outside the library. His face cleared when he caught sight of Webb.

"Sorry," Webb said. "Unavoidable delay."

"Not a very fruitful exercise, guv. The girls aren't close. I get the impression Arlette boasts a bit about her conquests, but no new names came up."

Webb grunted, trying to wrench his mind off Hannah. "I've got the address of two families she coaches. We'll follow them up later, and the stables she goes to. In the meantime we'll collect the car and get up to the university."

Edna was seated at the kitchen table, polishing silver and keeping up an endless stream of chatter. Claire had been edging towards the door for the last ten minutes, but had not yet managed to escape.

"So I said to her, 'Mrs. Davis, if you ask me, you brought it on yourself.' 'What do you mean, Edna?' she goes. 'Well,' I says, 'just think what you let her get away with. Stands to reason,' I says, 'she thinks she's got a free hand. After all—' "

Claire switched off, depending on intermittent nods of agreement to disguise her inattention. It was a unique relationship she shared with Edna, going back to the summer they were both ten years old, and the shy, thin child had watched her playing on her swing. As a result, Edna had a certain licence; reprimands had to be couched in such diplomatic language that Tom maintained only an expert in lateral thinking would realise one had been administered. A verbatim reporter, Edna was convinced of Claire's innate interest in all she said and did, and Claire hadn't the heart to disillusion her. Consequently, unless she made some excuse and left the house as soon as Edna arrived, Tuesday and Friday mornings were a write-off.

" '—and if you don't put your foot down,' I says, 'you mark my words, Mrs. Davis, your Sandra'll be no better than that flighty young French miss they're all looking for, and you wouldn't want that, now would you?' "

Claire's attention snapped back. "What did you say?"

Edna paused gratefully for breath, pushing her glasses into position with a polish-blackened finger. "Well, Miss

Claire, I felt it was time to speak plain. That young Sandra needs her bottom spanking, if you ask me."

"The French girl," Claire interrupted. "You know about her?"

"It's in all the papers, isn't it? Of course, I hope no harm comes to her, but carrying on like that she was asking for it, in my opinion."

Claire was very still. "Carrying on like what?"

Edna sniffed. "No better than she should be, if you ask me. I've seen her several times around the town, always with a different lad in tow. Oh, she *looked* proper enough, I grant you—except when she was in the car that time."

"What car? When?"

"Lord love us, Miss Claire, how do I know? A week or two back, at least."

"Where was the car?"

"In Farthing Lane, just up from Mrs. King's."

Claire's mouth was dry. *Simon*'s car? Her brief panic subsided. No, Simon's car was distinctive, to say the least, and Edna knew it well. An ancient and battered sports car in several shades of green, Sarah had christened it *The Hesperus*, and the name stuck. It was safe to ask, "Did you see who the man was?"

Edna sniffed again, disapproval on her face. "I've got better things to do than spy on courting couples. Anyway, I could only see the back of his head—though come to think of it, he'd got a bald patch on top. I remember thinking he was older than her usual. Shouldn't be surprised if he was married."

Was the information worth passing to Simon? It sounded very vague.

"Anyway," Edna continued, reverting to her original theme, "you don't expect any different of foreigners, but you don't want a local girl to go that way, do you?"

Claire hoped devoutly that Edna's opinion of local girls would never be diminished. "No," she agreed prudently, "you certainly don't."

The campus of Broadshire University was landscaped to take advantage of its unique position. From the main Bridge Road, a long driveway wound through rows of trees, with frequent paths that lead off signposted to different halls of residence—West Park, Avon, Somerset. As they drove, they continually passed groups of students with satchels and bundles of books under their arms, making their way either to or from the main faculty buildings. Eventually the avenue of trees opened into a large space like the centre of a village.

"Doesn't mention the French Department," Jackson said, peering at the different arms of the signpost.

"It'll be the arts building," Webb told him, primed by Marshbanks.

"What's French got to do with drawing?" Jackson demanded, but he turned the car in the direction indicated and they drove into the carpark. Inside the building, they approached the porter's desk and the man looked up from his newspaper.

"Yes, gentlemen? What can I do for you?"

"Chief Inspector Webb and Sergeant Jackson. We'd like a word with Professor Warwick, if it's convenient."

"Ah, you've come about Miss Picard, I suppose. Worrying business. You want the French corridor, sir. Up those stairs and through the swing doors on your left. The secretaries will help you."

However, when they reached the first floor, it was to learn that the professor was lecturing. Webb asked instead for Mr. Duncan.

He was a broad-shouldered Scot in his mid-thirties, with a thatch of dark hair and a small beard. He did not seem overjoyed to see them.

"There's not much I can tell you," he began discouragingly as they seated themselves. "I hardly know Miss Picard. I can't imagine why you think I can help you."

"She mentioned your name, sir," Webb said stolidly.

The man looked alarmed. "To whom?"

"A girlfriend."

"I can't think why. She sometimes sits at my table in the refectory, but I've no other contact with her."

"What's your impression of her?"

"Och, she's a bright enough girl. Cheerful and friendly."

"Any particular friends?"

He shrugged. "Charlie Peterson, Mike Partridge—" His voice tailed off.

"Do you ever see her off the campus, sir?"

Duncan flushed. "I'm a married man, Chief Inspector. With children."

Webb smiled slightly. "That hardly answers my question."

"I thought it did. But if you want it more plainly, no, I do not see her outside working hours. And hardly at all during them."

I'm not sure I believe you, Webb thought. The man was quite presentable and Arlette herself much sought after. It would be natural for them to come together. Yet he couldn't probe further in the face of such firm denial. Not yet, anyway. He tried another tack.

"Where were you, sir, between 10 A.M. and 2 P.M. on Tuesday?"

The flush deepened. "Why?"

"Because that's the time we're interested in."

"As it happens, I'd a dental appointment at eleven." He looked at them belligerently. "If I'd known she was going missing, I'd have changed it."

"And your dentist is—?"

For a moment, Webb thought he'd refuse to reply. But he sullenly gave name and address.

"And you came straight back here afterwards?"

"No. The surgery's not far from where I live, so I went home for lunch. As my wife will verify."

Jackson marvelled that anyone could still think a wife's evidence would exonerate him.

"So what time did you get back, sir?"

"About two. I'd a tutorial at two-fifteen."

Webb nodded without comment. "Did Miss Picard mention being homesick, or any family worries?"

"Certainly not to me."

Webb felt the wall of the man's resistance. Was it merely a clash of personalities, or had he something to hide? He said easily and with no inflection of irony, "Thank you very much for your time, Mr. Duncan. You've been most helpful."

"Like a stone giving blood," added Jackson, as the door closed behind them.

"Not everyone appreciates us, Ken. A policeman's lot, and all that."

"If you ask me he's been having it off with her. See how red he went?"

"Let's not jump to conclusions. If we need to come back, we will, never fear."

Arnold Lightbody was a different proposition. In his late forties, he wore thick pebble spectacles. He had tufts of straw-like hair round the sides of his head, but his high forehead stretched back as far as his crown. He smiled continually, showing yellow teeth.

"Well now, gentlemen," he began, before Webb could say anything, "you're worried about our little Arlette. So are we all."

"I'll be grateful for anything you can tell us, sir."

"A charming girl. Most attractive, if you understand me. And very popular."

"With women too?"

Lightbody smirked. "Now that you ask me," he said coyly, "I should say the young ladies are less enthusiastic. Possibly because she has the male population eating out of her hand."

"Including you, Dr. Lightbody?"

Lightbody laughed merrily, stopping when the policemen remained serious. "I'm a little old for that kind of thing, Inspector. No, I was referring to post-graduates. Her contemporaries."

"And the other tutors?"

"Dear me, I never thought of that. I suppose it's possible."

While appearing to give them full co-operation, Lightbody told them very little. He had apparently been on campus throughout the crucial time on Tuesday. Like Duncan, he claimed surprise that Arlette should have spoken of him.

Somewhat dispiritedly, the policemen made their way outside and stood for a moment looking about them. Ahead of them was the administrative building, and beyond it, grassy banks sloped fairly steeply down to the river. On the opposite bank, the old town basked in the spring sunshine, its Cotswold stone glowing cream and gold.

"Do these kids know how lucky they are?" Jackson asked rhetorically. "A bit different from Leyton Road Grammar! I never knew what I was missing." He turned to Webb with a grin, his envy vanishing. "Mind, I know what I'm missing now, and that's food! Any good pubs hereabouts, guv?"

"I think we'll try *The Barley Mow.* It's that grain barge moored on the quayside. All the young bloods frequent it—we might learn something to our advantage. Look," he added, "there's Sergeant Hopkins. Let's have a quick word."

The gloomy-faced sergeant, with a young constable beside him, had just emerged from the faculty building and turned towards the carpark. Webb and Jackson quickened their footsteps to catch up with them.

"Good morning, Sergeant. How's it going?"

Hopkins nodded a surly greeting. "Not too bad, sir. We managed to track down a couple of names on your list, with leads to the others."

"Anything of interest?"

"Hard to tell. They don't seem unduly worried. Think she's probably gone off on a whim and will turn up when it suits her."

"Has she done that before?"

Hopkins shrugged, but the young constable spoke up, blushing as he did so. "I think it's just that she's such a cheerful girl, sir. People can't imagine anything happening to her."

"Let's hope they're right," Webb said grimly. "You going back to Maybury Street?" Hopkins nodded. "Tell DI Ledbetter I've seen Duncan and Lightbody, and will be in touch later."

There was nowhere near the barge to park the car. They left it by the viaduct and walked back along the riverside, enjoying the sun on the water and the warmth of it on their backs. Children ran, calling, along the narrow path towards them, a small dog yapping at their heels, and on their left some half-dozen cottages nestled into the hillside, their neat little gardens blazing with flowers. On the far side of the river, the grass bank reached up towards the buildings they'd just left, its green expanse dotted with colour as groups of students relaxed in the sunshine or ate an *alfresco* lunch.

As they neared the pub, the path widened into biscuit-coloured cobbles and there were tables with umbrellas and groups of people eating and drinking.

"We'll hear more if we go inside," Webb murmured, and they walked together up the gangplank and into the little boat.

A wide, polished staircase led below into what had once been the hold of the barge. Jackson followed Webb down and looked about him approvingly. The conversion was imaginative, keeping a nautical flavour while providing a pleasant and unique bar, with tables round the walls beneath the small round portholes. On the walls were framed prints of barges and steamboats, and at the end hung a lifebelt with the name "Barley Mow" painted on it, flanked by port and starboard lamps. The room was filled with a laughing, chattering crowd of customers.

Webb and Jackson hitched themselves onto bar stools, ordering beer and cornish pasties. A burst of laughter sounded from the table immediately behind them as some ribald joke reached its conclusion. The average age of the clientele was well below thirty, Webb guessed, and he felt more conspicuous than he'd have liked. Then, as the crowd behind lapsed into brief silence, a girl's voice reached them from another table.

"The fuzz were up at the Uni this morning—did you know?"

Webb slid off his stool and moved further down the bar, ostensibly to help himself to cruet.

"About Arlette?" asked another voice. "Do you think something's happened to her?"

"God knows. If it has, my money's on Jane! I thought she'd kill her there and then, when she waltzed off with Mike!"

"You can laugh," said the second girl, "but it sounds pretty serious to me. Someone said her parents are coming over."

The noisy table had started up again, blotting out any further comment. Webb caught the bartender's eye, saw that his eavesdropping had been noted.

"You know this girl that's gone missing?" His hand moved to his breast pocket for identification, but the man waved it aside.

"I know who you are, mate. Yes, I've seen her. She's often in here."

"When was the last time?"

"Sunday, I reckon. Lunchtime."

"Was she with anyone in particular?"

The man shrugged. "Hard to tell. There was a crowd of them. Six or seven, mostly blokes."

"Any names?"

"Didn't register any—except Daisy, a little dark girl who's usually with them."

"And you've not seen the French girl since?"

"No. Monday's my day off and she wasn't in Tuesday. Two lads were talking about her, though. One of them had seen her in the town, and said she wasn't coming."

Webb leant forward. "He'd *seen* her? On Tuesday?"

The barman looked surprised. "That's right."

"You're quite sure?"

"Yeah. It was quiet in here at the time. I heard him quite clearly."

"He didn't say where he'd seen her?"

"Don't think so, but I wasn't paying much attention. Hold on a moment. That's the lad, over there."

Webb turned quickly, saw a dark young man, pint mug in hand, leaning against a wall and talking to a girl.

"And that's her, and all," added the barman eagerly. "That's Daisy."

Webb put down his fork and edged his way through the crowd, Jackson falling in behind him.

"Excuse me."

The man turned and his brows lifted. "Police?"

"That's right, sir. Webb, Shillingham CID."

The young man nodded. "I know Simon Marshbanks. I'm Peter Campbell, and this is Daisy Drew."

The girl nodded nervously.

"The barman tells me you saw Arlette Picard on Tuesday morning. Is that right?"

"Quite right. Is it important?"

"It could be."

"Well, she didn't say much. She was in a hurry—said she was meeting someone."

"Where and when was this, sir?"

"About ten-thirty, I suppose, outside the library. I was going to visit a client—I'm an accountant."

"Did she say who she was meeting?"

Campbell looked rueful. "No, she wouldn't tell me."

"You mean you asked her, and she refused to tell you?"

"Not exactly refused. She just laughed and shook her head."

"And she didn't say where she was going?"

"No."

If she'd been in a hurry then, it was nothing to do with Marshbanks. Their date was for the afternoon.

"What direction was she going in?"

"Towards Gloucester Road." Campbell paused and added sombrely, "Was I the last person to see her? I never thought."

"The last we've traced so far, by twenty minutes. How did she seem?"

"Full of the joys, as usual. Oh, she did say, 'Simon's taking me to see the horses later.' I remember thinking, Good old Simon, stealing a march on me again." He finished his drink. "If there's nothing else, I'd better get back to the office."

Webb nodded. "We have your address, if we need you. And you, Miss Drew," he added, as Campbell patted the girl on the shoulder and moved away. "Do you know anyone Miss Picard was in the habit of meeting?"

Daisy shook her head, but Webb felt she knew something. He said more gently, "She might be in danger, you know. You won't get anyone into trouble who doesn't deserve to be."

"There was really only the crowd we go round with: Steve, Mike, Charlie, and Alan." She wasn't meeting his eyes.

"There's someone else, isn't there?" But she would not be drawn.

"Very well," Webb said heavily. "If you remember anything, you can get me at the police station."

"Bet you it's Duncan the Bruce she was thinking of," Jackson said, as they came up the stairs again into the sunshine.

"Might be, but we couldn't press her any more. Now"—he looked at his watch—"we've just time to report back before we meet that train."

CHAPTER 4

At ten past three that afternoon, Jackson parked the car in the station forecourt and he and Webb went into the booking hall. A tall, dark-haired man with a slight stoop came towards them.

"Good afternoon, gentlemen. I take it you're the police? Bernard Warwick, Broadshire University. Sorry to have missed you earlier."

Webb took his hand, introducing himself.

"From Shillingham?" The professor raised an eyebrow.

"The local police asked for assistance, sir. They're understrength at the moment, due to an accident."

"And have you any news of this girl?"

"Not so far, I'm afraid. We're tracing everyone who has any contact with her, but it's a slow business. Do you know her yourself?"

"Only by sight. I've had no direct dealings with her."

The three men walked slowly out onto the platform. "I'm not looking forward to this," Webb said frankly. "I'm glad you're here, sir. I don't speak the lingo and there's no saying how good their English will be."

"I'll do what I can," the professor said smoothly. Webb glanced sideways at him. It was an oddly unexpressive face, and although the man had met his eyes as they shook hands, his own had given nothing away. Webb sensed an iron self-discipline and pondered the necessity for it.

In the distance the yellow disc of the engine appeared. The three men straightened and stood waiting. The train was a through one to Gloucester, and not many alighted here, but by coincidence they were opposite the right door.

Catching sight of the couple standing there, Webb braced himself—no hysterics, please God—and beside him heard Warwick also draw in his breath.

The woman in the doorway looked to be in shock. There was a murmur from behind her as her husband urged her forward, but, having arrived, she seemed reluctant to step from the train. Webb moved forward and took her arm. "Permit me, madame." (Surely, he hoped, the same in any language.) Her husband handed down his cases to Jackson, and as he stepped after his wife onto the platform, the guard blew his whistle and the train moved away. Webb turned for help to the professor, but the man seemed as much at a loss as himself.

"My colleague and I are from the police," he said perforce, speaking slowly and distinctly. "We very much regret the reason for your visit, and assure you we're doing all in our power to find your daughter."

The Frenchman nodded in general understanding. "Professor Warwick?" Webb prompted. The man moved forward at last and launched into a fluent stream of French. The woman kept her eyes on him as he spoke, but her husband's fell away, and to his disquiet Webb noticed they were wet. As Warwick stopped speaking, the group turned by mutual consent and walked back to the car. Webb saw that a dark blue Porsche was parked at the far side of the forecourt—no doubt the professor's. He said in a low voice, "It would be better if they went in your car, Professor, since you can speak to each other. We'll see you at the hotel."

Warwick turned. "I'm sorry, Chief Inspector, I have to get back now. I've explained that you'll look after them."

Webb stared at him. "But, sir, we can't conduct an interview without you! That was the point of your being here."

A tactical slip, as he immediately realised. "On the contrary," the professor said coldly, "I'm representing the university as a matter of courtesy, but you're in charge of the case, and interviews are police business. I certainly haven't time to attend them." He nodded formally to the French couple and strode to his car.

"Bloody hell!" Jackson said under his breath. "What now, guv?"

Webb, aware of his own inability to deal with the visitors, held down his anger. "We'll take them to the hotel, and phone for an interpreter. It's a bloody waste of time, but it can't be helped." He turned to the French parents. "Forgive me. We were under the impression the professor was coming with us. If you'd like to get into the car—?"

Jackson, having put the cases in the boot, was holding open the rear door, and as the couple bent to step inside, Webb was able to take a longer look at them. The woman was small and dark. Her hair, which even he could tell had been expertly cut, had touches of silver at the temples, an effect which paradoxically made her face look younger. Now, she was pale and strained-looking, her huge brown eyes dark-circled, but she was still a very attractive woman. It was from her husband, fair and blue-eyed, that their daughter took her colouring.

But what the hell was he going to do with them? God knew how long it would take to get an interpreter from the university. Might Chris Ledbetter know of one? However long it took, he and Jackson would have to stay with the Picards till someone came. Firstly because they needed all the information they could get, and secondly on humanitarian grounds.

He glowered out of the window as Jackson drove towards the hotel. A set of traffic lights changed to red as they approached, and Webb drummed his fingers impatiently, staring out at the imposing stone building alongside, which a board informed him was a gallery of modern art. And at the familiar figure coming down the steps.

In the same instant he flung open the car door. "Wait a minute!" he threw over his shoulder, and then, "Hannah!" She raised her head, stopping in surprise, and waited for him to reach her.

"Hannah, thank God! You speak French, don't you?" Rapidly he told her his problem.

"How long will it take?" she asked doubtfully. "I have to collect the girls in an hour."

"Not long, I promise, but for God's sake help us out. The poor devils haven't a clue what's happening."

"All right."

With a sigh of thankfulness he hurried her over to the car. "This lady owns a school," he said inaccurately, judging the subtleties of deputy Headmistress beyond his listeners. "She will assist us." He was speaking, he felt, like a textbook, in his efforts to make himself clear. Then, blessedly, Hannah with her warm smile took over her own introduction, conveying, as far as he could make out, her sympathy, and offering her help.

"Sorry not to introduce you," he said *sotto voce* to Jackson over the flow of soft French behind them. "Miss James—"

"I met her at Westridge," Jackson said.

"So you did. I was forgetting." The nursery-rhyme case. The memory of it was inextricably woven with Susan.

They turned off the road by the sign of The White Swan, and Jackson pulled into the hotel carpark.

"It might be better to talk in the lounge," Webb said, as the French couple signed the register. "There's no one about, and we could have some tea. It would help to ease the proceedings."

The Picards, approached through Hannah, agreed to the plan, though Madame requested chocolate and her husband coffee. Foreigners! thought Jackson.

The interview fell into its own pattern. Webb asked the questions, Hannah translated, Monsieur replied—nearly always Monsieur. He had the sensitive face of a poet, with a high forehead and hollow cheeks. A gentle-looking man, Webb thought, trying to come to terms with the sudden crisis in his life. His wife, pale and on edge, sat for the most part in silence, though it appeared she understood a modicum of English. Such replies as she did make came before

Hannah translated. As to the answers, they were not much help. No, Arlette had never gone off before. No, they had no idea where she might be. No, there was no serious boyfriend in France. Yes, she had mentioned names in her letters, but not one more than the others, and her parents hadn't registered them.

The requested photograph was produced and at last Webb looked on the face of Arlette Picard. The full mouth and tip-tilted nose gave her a provocative air. The fair hair formed a softly fuzzy halo round her head, the blue eyes laughed at the camera.

"We'll need it for the press," Webb said. "I presume they'll let us keep it?"

Madame nodded. "*Bien sûr*, monsieur."

"Will you explain," Webb said awkwardly to Hannah, "that we'll keep them advised of any developments, but in the meantime there's not much they can do."

Madame nodded again and replied in French, "We just wanted to be here."

"Then we won't keep you any longer. I'll ask Professor Warwick to put someone who speaks French at your disposal, and do please contact us if there's anything we can do." He scrawled the Maybury Street phone number on the back of his own card and handed it across. With a formal shaking of hands all round, the French couple left them to be shown upstairs to their room.

Webb turned back to Hannah, conscious of Jackson's interest. "Miss James, I don't know what we'd have done without you. Thank you very much indeed."

"I'm glad to have been of help."

"The least I can do is run you up to the university." He looked at the clock above the reception desk. "You have twenty minutes in hand."

"Oh, don't worry, I can—"

"The least I can do," he repeated, and turned to Jackson. "Sergeant, will you go on to Maybury Street and report to Inspector Ledbetter? I'll drop Miss James off and join you there. I want a word with the professor, but I'd better calm down before I approach him. In any case, if he hadn't time for the interview, he won't spare any for me."

The car, which had been standing in the sun, was unbearably stuffy. Webb opened all the windows, took off his jacket, and tossed it on the back seat. "Perhaps we'll have a hot summer for once."

Hannah wasn't listening. "Do you think she's still alive, David?"

"I don't know. The more time that passes, the less likely it seems."

He started the car. It was like old times to be discussing a case with Hannah, but he knew better than to say so. At least this second meeting had helped to thaw the atmosphere. He'd go and see her one evening, as soon as he could make it. Now they'd established contact again, she might let him plead his case. It felt unbelievably good to have her beside him as the car climbed steeply up the hill, with the breeze from the open windows lifting their hair. God, he'd missed her—was still missing her.

"Where shall I drop you?"

"The admin building, please. You know where it is?"

"Yes, I ferreted my way round this morning. It's a town in itself, isn't it? Theatre, shops, bank, chapel. How many actually live up here?"

"About a thousand, I think. The rest are scattered round the town and villages in digs or rented houses."

"You think your girls will plump for it, or has somewhere further afield more glamour?"

"It depends what courses are on offer."

Webb smiled. "Me, I'm no academic. I'd come for the view alone."

"It's marvellous, isn't it? You should paint it. You'd have a ready market here."

"It's a thought." He turned to her. "Thanks again, Hannah. I really appreciate your help."

"That's all right." She swung gracefully out of the car. "Goodbye, David. Thanks for the lift."

He watched her until she disappeared through the swing doors into the building, then he turned the car and drove back to the town.

Despite the open window, the bedroom was hot with the day's stored sunshine. Beside her, Tom slept peacefully, occasionally emitting a bubbling little snore.

Restlessly Claire turned on her side. Across the silent town the church clock chimed sonorously and she counted the strokes: one, two, three. What a horrible hour to be awake! All the worries she could suppress during daylight seemed to leap out at her, assuming monstrous proportions. Mainly she thought of Arlette. Her parents would have arrived by now. Were they, too, awake, listening to the same clock strike?

Involuntarily, Claire pictured herself in their position, in some strange French town where Sarah was missing. She put her hands to her head to squeeze out the thought.

Who was the older man Edna'd seen with Arlette? She *should* have told Simon. She'd phone him tomorrow. Oh, *please* let the girl turn up safely, and they could all get some sleep.

She turned again, her cotton nightdress sticking to her body. The airlessness of the room suffocated her. Despite deep breaths, she seemed unable to fill her lungs.

Carefully so as not to disturb Tom, she slid off the bed and padded to the window, silently pushing up the sash and leaning out as far as she could. A faint night breeze was cool on her forehead and damp shoulders. She closed her eyes, breathing deeply. Then she opened them, letting them move over the silver and black garden beneath her.

Their bedroom was at the back of the house, and Claire loved its daytime outlook—the patio directly below with the plants in its edging wall, the splash of geraniums in their tubs, and the flowering shrubs further up the garden, following one another in colourful sequence from spring to autumn. Now, colour was drained away, leaving only light and shade, like an old television set.

Far above her, the sky was speckled with stars. She lifted her head, letting the breeze play over her throat. That was better. Perhaps she'd sleep now. Idly she turned her head to the left, towards the Warwicks' garden—and froze, her fingers clamped on the sill. In the centre of the lawn a figure stood motionless. It must have been there as long as she had—she'd been aware of no movement. A burglar? But why so still? Then, as her eyes focussed, she saw it was Bernard, standing with his head flung back as though gazing into the top branches of the trees at the foot of the garden. Had he heard or seen something? What was he *doing* out there at three in the morning, in his pyjamas and dressing-gown?

The breeze felt suddenly chill and Claire shivered. Slowly, so as not to attract his attention—though he was facing away from her—she withdrew inside the window. For a moment she stood hugging herself, stroking her cool bare arms as though for comfort. Perhaps he couldn't sleep, either. But—outside? And how long had he been there?

She went to the bathroom for a glass of water and drank it slowly, sip by sip. By the time she got back to her room, he'd have gone. But when, almost fearfully, she again looked out of the window, he was still there, seeming not to have moved since she'd last seen him. Shivering and perplexed, Claire crept back to bed.

Saturday morning, and Webb was seated at his desk, looking through some reports before leaving for Steeple Bayliss. There was a knock on the door and young Marshbanks looked round it.

"Come in, Simon. What is it?"

"It might not be important, sir, but my mother's just been on. She says her daily help saw Arlette with a man in a car."

"When?"

"A week or two ago. They were parked near her digs.

Edna can't describe the car—it was dark, and she's not really up on cars anyway. But she saw the back of the man's head, and he had a bald patch."

"Anything else?"

"Afraid not, sir."

"Well, we'll look into it. Thanks, Simon. Ask Sergeant Jackson to come in, would you?"

Jackson knocked and entered, his china-blue eyes less bright than usual. Webb grinned at him sympathetically. "You look as though you've been out on the tiles, Ken."

"Not exactly the tiles. Millie had a false alarm during the night. I whipped her into hospital and hung around for an hour or so. Then they came and said she's a while to go yet, so I took her home. In a way, I'd rather they'd kept her in. She'd get more rest there."

"When are the babies due?"

"Tomorrow's the date we were given, but you never know."

"Well, if she's a while to go, it won't be today. Sit down a minute. I've been going through the reports of the SB team which we collected last night. They've managed to trace a few of Arlette's admirers, but that's as far as it goes. However, according to Simon she was seen with an older man, so we'll have a look at the fathers of the kids she's been coaching and the rest of the tutors. What did you think of the two we saw yesterday?"

"Not much. Lightbody was a bit *too* co-operative—smarmy, almost. And those little eyes behind the glasses. They didn't miss a trick."

"You think he might fancy Arlette?"

"I wouldn't be surprised. I can see him smacking his lips over a bit of skirt. Still, that doesn't make him a killer."

"You reckon that's what we're looking for?"

Jackson met his eyes squarely. "Don't you?"

Webb drummed his fingers on the desk without replying. Then he said, "What about Duncan?"

Jackson grinned. "Typical Scot. Gave nothing away, even

information. But if it was a two-way thing, he's the more likely bet."

"Hm. I also intend to have a word with the professor this morning, whether he thinks he can spare the time or not. What did you make of *him?*"

"A rum egg, wasn't he? Like a dummy in a tailor's window."

"He's living on his nerves. You can almost feel him vibrating."

"I don't reckon him for any hanky-panky, though. From the look of him, he wouldn't know where to start."

Webb thought of Jackson's description when, two hours later, they were seated opposite Professor Warwick in his study. Not so much a dummy, he thought, as a robot, whose inner workings were whirring out of control. He'd the uneasy impression that it was several seconds before Warwick had realised who he was. Then his computer-brain reasserted itself.

"You're lucky to find me here on a Saturday, Chief Inspector. I have some work to finish." His mouth moved in what was intended as a smile. "I'm sorry you felt I deserted you yesterday. A misunderstanding, apparently."

"I certainly assumed you'd help with the interview," Webb said levelly. "However, we were able to make other arrangements."

"So I gather."

"Oh?"

"Madame Picard phoned for an appointment. She's coming to see me in ten minutes, but I'm free until then."

Webb had finished with him within that time. As he'd indicated the previous day, Warwick seemed to have had few dealings with Arlette. "Thank you for your help," Webb finished. "And we'd better have your address, in case we need to contact you."

"14 Lime Tree Grove." It sounded familiar, though Webb couldn't think why. They took their leave, and as they approached the swing doors at the end of the corridor, Madame Picard came hesitantly through them.

"Good morning, madame. You're looking for Professor Warwick?"

She nodded, returning his greeting with a murmured "*Bonjour.*"

"The far door on the left. Shall I—?"

"No—please. I—shall manage." She gave him a brief nod and smile and walked quickly down the length of the corridor.

"I hope he apologises for dashing off like that," Webb commented. "The French are sticklers for politeness."

Jackson had other things on his mind. "Guv, that address the professor gave. Doesn't Simon Marshbanks live in Lime Tree Grove?"

"My God, you're right, Ken! I knew it rang a bell. We'll give him a buzz when we get to Maybury Street."

"Next door?" Webb repeated over the phone. "Your people live next door to the professor?" He knew Marshbanks came from a wealthy family, but to find him in such elevated surroundings was a surprise. "Do you know him?" He listened intently for a few minutes, made a number of comments, and rang off.

"That could be useful," he told Ledbetter and Jackson, who'd been listening to the one-sided conversation. "Marshbanks' parents and the Warwicks are friends. It might help to get a personal slant on the po-faced professor. And since we also need to follow up the info from the daily, I reckon a call is indicated. Phone through, Ken, and see when it would be convenient to pop in. But first, we'll call on the families Arlette coached. They should be home on a Saturday morning."

CHAPTER 5

Later, Webb reflected ruefully that a bit of judicious eavesdropping at the professor's door would have saved them a lot of trouble. For as he and Jackson returned to Maybury Street, Cécile Picard and Bernard Warwick confronted each other across a gulf of thirty years.

For some moments they stood gripping each other's hands, too emotional for words. Then Bernard spoke softly in French. "It really is true, then. When I saw you, at the train door—"

"Yes. For a moment I thought I should faint."

"It's unbelievable, meeting after all these years. Fate, obviously."

Her fingers moved protestingly in his. "Arlette rather than fate, *mon cher.*" She gave a little shudder. "You think she is all right, Bernard? We will find her?"

"God willing, my love."

She didn't register the endearment. "I'm so frightened," she said in a low voice, "and Gaston—"

"Ah yes, the worthy Gaston. How did you give him the slip?"

"I—beg your pardon?"

"It would have been natural, surely, for him to come here with you?" His voice sharpened. "He doesn't know?"

She shook her head. "No, no. I said nothing. What purpose would it serve?" She moved away from him, walking to the window and looking down over the bustling, sunlit world of the campus. "He is not strong, my husband. Today he suffers with migraine. Strain always affects him that way." Her voice sank, and he moved closer to catch what she was saying. "I heard him in the night, weeping hopelessly."

Bernard said sharply, "He should put a brave face on it, for your sake."

She turned with a smile. "I had forgotten how English you are. But yes, it is necessary to hide my fears, to avoid adding to his."

Bernard caught her hand, gripping it painfully. "You have me now, *mignonne*, and I'm strong. You can lean on me."

She closed her eyes briefly, letting the reassurance of his strength flow through her. Then, gently, she removed her hand.

"My dear, we parted as lovers, but we meet now as friends. I am married to a good man and have four children. What was between us ended thirty years ago." He started to speak, but she continued quickly, "And you also are married, and have children?"

"No children." He spoke roughly and she frowned, eyes searching his face. "I married only ten years ago. It was a mistake. If I'd waited—"

"No, no," she interrupted. "You must not think like that."

He said jerkily, "I went straight back, you know, after the quarrel. On the next boat. But you'd vanished completely. Your parents said you'd left Paris and wanted nothing more to do with me. I argued and begged, but they wouldn't tell me where you were."

She said quietly, "I'd no idea. They said nothing to me."

He shrugged. "None of our friends knew your whereabouts, and it's been the same ever since. I go back each year, walking the streets we walked, sitting in the same cafés. And I ask everyone I see—concierges, barmen, even gendarmes—if they know of you. They never do."

She said gently, "I left Paris when you did, to stay with my aunt in Angers. I met Gaston almost immediately, and we married six months later."

"On the rebound."

"Perhaps. But I love him, Bernard, as you love your wife."

He shook his head vehemently. "I have never loved anyone else, nor shall I. And now that I've found you—"

She said quickly, "I came to speak of Arlette. Please, my dear. I can think of nothing else."

"Of course. We'll wait till she's found before we tell them."

She stared at him, perplexed, then abandoned the attempt to understand him. "Tell me, when did you see her last? Was she well?"

With an effort he controlled himself. He mustn't add to her worries as her husband was doing. After thirty years, he could wait a few more days. His habitual restraint came to his aid, his breathing steadied, and he smiled at her.

"Sit down, my dear. I'll ring for coffee, then I'll tell you all I know about your daughter."

As the police car drew up, Rob Palfry was playing a hose over the gleaming car in his driveway. He turned, his eyes narrowed against the sun, surprised by the unexpected visitors. Webb took in his appearance in one swift, experienced glance. Medium height, slightly over-weight, thinning brown hair. The arms below the short-sleeved shirt were muscular and strong.

"Can I help you?" he asked warily, as Webb and Jackson approached.

"I hope so, sir." Webb identified himself. "We're inquiring into the disappearance of Miss Arlette Picard."

"Oh God, yes," Palfry said, and flushed.

"You know her, I believe?"

"Not personally, but my children do. She gives them French lessons."

"Could we have a word with them?"

"I suppose so. Just a minute, I'll call my wife." He paused, added rather unwillingly, "You'd better come inside."

The policemen followed him up the path, the gravel dazzling in the midday sun. He pushed open the front door and called, "Liz! Can you come?"

"Not at the moment," came the reply. "Why do you always want me when I'm covered in flour?"

Palfry glanced at the silent men beside him, walked quickly to the kitchen, and pushed open the door. "The police are here," he said shortly.

"The *police?*"

"About Arlette."

"Oh God, she isn't—?"

"She isn't anything, as far as I know, but they want to speak to us. All of us. Where are the twins?"

"I don't know. Una was practising a minute ago. She's probably gone outside."

There was a sound of running water, then her husband moved aside and she came into the hall. Webb repeated his introduction and Mrs. Palfry nodded nervously. She had unusually black hair in a ragged urchin cut, and was wearing jeans and a T-shirt.

"I think the girls are outside," she said. "Do come in—fancy keeping you standing in the hall!" She threw a reproving glance at her husband and opened a door on the left. They all moved inside. Beyond the open patio doors, two teenaged girls lounged in deck chairs on the still-shadowed patio. Their father called them indoors.

"The police, asking about Arlette. Our daughters, Una and Zoë." The girls, completely identical as far as Jackson could see, were as dark as their mother. They had asserted such individuality as they could by dressing differently, one in shorts and shirt, one in dungarees and top. They looked about seventeen. Jackson studied them, his eyes moving from one small, pointed face to the other. Twins fascinated him. Would his own be boys or girls? And, oh God, how was Millie? He'd ring her during the lunch break.

"Now, tell us all you can about Miss Picard," Webb began, when they were all seated. "How long has she been coming here?"

"Since before Christmas." It was Mrs. Palfry who replied. "She put an advertisement in the local newsagents, and since the girls have A-levels coming up, it seemed a good idea to give them a booster."

"How often does she come?"

"Every Thursday, for two hours."

The usual questions followed. Had she spoken of any friends, any plans she might have made? Apparently she had not.

Webb said casually, "Do you run her home afterwards, Mr. Palfry?"

The man started and flushed again. "No, I do not," he said emphatically. "She's old enough to look after herself." He paused, realised the inappropriateness of his words, and added lamely, "Anyway, it's less than five minutes' walk."

"So you know where she lives?"

"She—mentioned it once."

"I thought you hadn't met her?"

"I didn't say I hadn't *met* her." There were beads of sweat on his upper lip, and one of the twins giggled nervously. Her father glared at her. "I said I don't *know* her, and that's the truth."

"So she's never been in your car, for example?"

"Look, what is this? How many times do I—"

"Purely routine, sir. I presume you've no objection if we examine it? We'll try not to inconvenience you."

The man stared at him, his deep colour ebbing away to leave his skin pasty white. He shook his head without speaking.

"You've just been cleaning it, I see. Inside as well as out?"

Palfry moistened his lips. "I—took the brush and dustpan to it."

"Well, please don't do any more. Someone will collect it this afternoon. We won't keep it longer than we have to." He looked round the circle of anxious faces. "And if you think of anything else, you know where to find us."

"Any thoughts, Ken?" he asked, as they drove out of Westfield Road.

"Well, it surprised me, you asking for the car. Bit early for that, isn't it?"

"In the normal way, yes. But he seemed jumpy, and he *had* been hosing it down. OK, so a lot of men clean their cars on Saturdays. Call it a shot in the dark, to see how he'd react."

"He reacted all right. Got really hot under the collar."

"Yes. I wonder why."

"*And* he's got a bald patch."

Webb smiled. "Quite. We'll see what the SOCOs find."

Tewkesbury Close, the home of the Morgan family, was up Gloucester Road, towards the top of the hill. On the way they passed the turning to Lime Tree Grove. "Three o'clock at the Marshbanks'," Jackson commented. "I meant to tell you."

"Fine. When we've seen this lot, we'll stop for lunch."

"Back to the boat?"

"No, we'll try that place we've just passed, The Lamb and Flag. I could murder a pint right now."

The Morgan family reacted more calmly to the arrival of the police. The father was tall, wellbuilt—and balding. But damn it, thought Webb impatiently, so was half the male population of SB. His heavy lids and full mouth gave him a sensuous look which might have been misleading, and though he betrayed no anxiety, he seemed, Webb felt, to be keeping a tight rein on himself.

The mother was of little interest to the police, fair-haired and pleasant-looking, and the children, a boy and girl in their late teens, answered straightforwardly enough. Arlette came to the house on Monday evenings, from six o'clock till eight. Only when Webb raised the matter of a lift home did he sense a ripple of unease.

"Oh, certainly." Mrs. Morgan was answering. "Nigel always runs her back. It's a mile or more to her lodgings."

"I see." Webb looked at Morgan. The man's eyes flickered but did not drop. He decided to repeat his ploy. Scenes of Crime would bless him for this. "You won't object if we examine your car, sir?"

Morgan frowned. "Why should you want to? You've heard the girl's been in it."

"Just routine," Webb said soothingly. "When was the last time you saw her?"

He was still looking at Morgan, but it was his wife who replied. "Monday evening, as usual."

"And you took her home, sir?"

"I dropped her off, yes. I go on to bowls, so it's not out of my way. I play at the club every Monday."

"Did she seem any different from usual? Or mention any plans for the next day?"

But he knew the answer before he asked it. Either Arlette Picard kept her affairs to herself, or those in whom she confided had no intention of betraying such confidence.

"Right, Ken," Webb said resignedly, fastening his seat-belt, "The Lamb and Flag, next stop." He glanced at his sergeant's set face. "And you can ring Millie while we wait for the grub." He grinned. "Quite a coincidence, wasn't it, seeing twins? Hope yours aren't as alike as that—you'd never tell them apart."

"I don't care what they look like as long as they get a move on," Jackson said tensely. "Right, guv, The Lamb and Flag coming up. Let's hope they serve real ale."

Webb had vaguely supposed that had he been blessed with money, he'd have chosen to live in an old house. The Marshbanks obviously felt otherwise. Lime Tree Grove, high above the town, was a twelve-year-old development of what estate agents called "executive houses." The trees which gave the road its name stood at regular intervals along the kerb, and in addition a landscaped plot of grass, shrubs, and conifers filled the pavement alongside the Marshbanks' house. Number 14 was directly behind it.

Mr. Marshbanks opened the door, looking ridiculously like his son. Or vice versa. He had the same stocky figure, bright, boot-button eyes, and rosy complexion. He even had a double crown like Simon's, which ensured that a tuft of black hair stood upright, despite all attempts to flatten it.

"Delighted to meet you, Webb!" he said, warmly shaking the Chief Inspector's hand. "We know you well by name. Claire, the police are here."

Mrs. Marshbanks rose from a chair as they were shown into the sitting-room. As he took her hand, Webb felt an unexpected spurt of pleasure. There was something instantly attractive about Claire Marshbanks—in her welcoming smile, her brown eyes, her honey-blonde hair—that created a feeling of warmth. Here was a woman at peace with herself and her world. In other circumstances, he thought with a tinge of regret, they could have been friends. It was a lot to read into a smile and a handshake, but he was sure he was right.

"Do sit down." Her gesture included Jackson. "I've just made some tea. Would you like some?"

"Thank you."

As she busied herself pouring it, Webb studied the room. The colouring was subtle—cream walls, grey carpet, but the heavy curtains were a warm apricot, a colour repeated in the upholstered suite. Though the easy chairs were modern, they blended perfectly with the antique cabinets and occasional tables that dotted the room. Bowls of flowers stood everywhere, part of the overall decor, and original watercolours were displayed on three of the walls. Given the opportunity, he'd study those more closely.

The realisation that this understated luxury was home to his young constable, while he himself was cooped up in a small flat at the top of Beechcroft Mansions, brought a wry shaft of envy, as shortlived as it was unaccustomed. Because what the hell would he do with all this stuff, rattling round in a house this size?

"Now," Tom Marshbanks said briskly, as they sat back with their tea, "what can we do for you?"

It emerged from Webb's questions that Claire'd met Arlette, and he was glad to add her impressions to those already collected. She repeated Edna's story of the parked car and passed on her address; which ended the official part of the visit. Webb had no justification for introducing Warwick's name, other than professional curiosity and a gut feeling he couldn't put a name to. Nevertheless, leaning back in his chair, he said conversationally, "I believe Professor Warwick lives next door?"

To his surprise, Mrs. Marshbanks, refilling her husband's cup, jumped, and some liquid spilled in the saucer. "I'm sorry. How careless of me."

Webb glanced at her husband and caught his quick frown. "Are you close friends?" he asked, ignoring the interruption.

"My wife's on a committee with Mrs. Warwick," Marshbanks answered. "I don't know either of them well, though as it happens they're coming to dinner this evening."

"Then you get on well together?"

Marshbanks met his bland gaze. "Are you as casual as you're trying to imply, Chief Inspector?"

Webb smiled. "Almost, sir."

"But Bernard works at the same institution as Arlette. Is that it?"

"Exactly."

Marshbanks smiled slightly. "Well, you've met him. Does he strike you as the type to start up a dangerous liaison with one of his colleagues?"

"I can't say he does, sir." Webb paused, his eyes on Claire's averted face. "Forgive me, but Mrs. Marshbanks seemed startled when I mentioned him."

She raised her head. "It's too silly for words. Just that last night, I—" She stopped, flushed, and finished quickly, "I had a dream about him. It disturbed me, that's all."

It wasn't what she'd started out to say, Webb felt sure. What had really happened last night?

"Have they any family?"

"No, they've only been married ten years. They were late starters."

"Neither had been married before?"

"No."

"But they strike you as happy? Look," he added impulsively, "I apologise for grilling you about friends. I'm sure you realise it's necessary, and completely confidential."

"As I said, I don't know them well. Claire?"

"He seems a most devoted husband. Beryl thinks the world of him."

"Has he ever mentioned Arlette Picard in your hearing?"

She shook her head decidedly. "Never."

"Right. Then there's only one more question I have for you." He smiled suddenly, relaxing. "May I look at your superb watercolours?"

"Of course." Claire was as much taken aback by the smile as the request. Unlike his earlier, more perfunctory ones, it had transformed the rather hard face, with its bleak grey eyes and tight mouth, into a surprisingly attractive one. As she walked with him to the wall of paintings, she was aware of him for the first time as a man rather than a police officer, reassessing the plentiful brown hair, the loose, rangy body, and the unselfconscious height of him. This last appealed to her particularly; a tall woman herself, Claire was the same height as both her husband and her son, and it was an unaccustomed pleasure to be with someone who made her feel petite.

His knowledge of the paintings came as a surprise. Without hint of pretentiousness, he discussed easily with her the techniques of the various artists and the relative merits of their works.

"I'd no idea you were such an authority, Mr. Webb," she said with a laugh. "You should be conducting our Art Appreciation course!"

He looked embarrassed. "I hope my enthusiasm didn't run away with me. It's a hobby, that's all, but I'm certainly no expert."

Marshbanks spoke from behind them. "I thought cartoons were your forte, Chief Inspector?"

Webb turned with a rueful smile. "They're supposed to be incognito. Simon's powers of deduction, no doubt."

"What cartoons?" Claire was puzzled.

"In the Broadshire News. And very pertinent they are, too. Signed with an S in a circle." Marshbanks smilingly held Webb's eye.

"And no doubt that cipher's also been cracked?"

"A spider in a web."

"A *spider?*" Claire echoed.

"An unavoidable nick-name. One of the old lags started it, years ago. It's pretty widespread now."

Claire said, "That's fascinating, but cartoons are very different from watercolours. Do you paint as well?"

"Just as a hobby. Landscapes, mostly. It's a great form of relaxation."

"And you sell them, too?"

He laughed. "Good lord, no. I lose interest once they're finished, and bundle them into the loft."

"I'd be very interested to see them."

He shook his head. "Really, they're nothing special. Strictly for my own amusement." He looked across at Jackson, doodling on his notebook. "We must be on our way. Thank you for your help—and the tea."

"What a fascinating man," Claire said, when Tom returned from showing the policemen out. "You never told me about the cartoons."

"I thought you knew. Simon mentioned them one day, and since then I've looked out for them. He's got a real gift for caricature—the people he draws are instantly recognisable."

"I'd love to see his paintings. If they're as good as you say the cartoons are, he could be a real find. I wonder if we could persuade him to exhibit at Melbray?"

Marshbanks laughed protestingly. "Hold on, darling! He doesn't strike me as the type who'd welcome publicity."

Deciding to pursue the matter if the chance arose, Claire

thought back to the reason for the visit. "I hope Edna won't mind our sending the police round."

"Mind? She'll have a field day. You'll get a blow-by-blow account on Tuesday."

"They seemed interested in Bernard, too."

"An interest you fuelled by shying like a frightened pony."

"Yes, it was silly. I wasn't expecting it, that's all."

"Just because the poor chap fancied a breath of air—"

"At three in the morning?"

"You did yourself. You went to the window for it, he to the garden. What's the difference?"

"I suppose you're right. But if he'd been walking about it would have seemed more normal. He just didn't move at all, for at least ten minutes."

"Perhaps he was meditating. Anyway, get your reflexes under control before they come to dinner, or we're in for a sticky evening."

"By Jove, guv," Jackson commented as they drove back to Shillingham, "that cleaner woman was a talker, wasn't she? Took you all your time to get a word in."

"Better than having to keep prompting," Webb returned, "but she'd told Mrs. Marshbanks all she knew. And it boils down to the fact that Arlette had an older man in tow. So what? It doesn't make him any more suspect than the younger ones."

"My money's still on Duncan."

"It could be any of the tutors, come to that, or those fathers we saw this morning. Palfry over-reacted, and Morgan, though he was calm enough, had a shifty look about him. He *could* be a leading pillar of the community, but if I'd a daughter, I wouldn't let him within sight of her. They might all warrant another visit, specially since nothing's coming out of the house to house. For the moment we're well and truly stymied."

Jackson said diffidently, "Well, as long as we *are* stymied, guv, would it be OK if I took tomorrow off? Millie—"

"Yes, of course, Ken." Webb smiled. "As a matter of fact, my chat with Mrs. Marshbanks put me in the mood for sketching. I might snatch a couple of hours myself, if things stay quiet."

There was something else he wanted to do during the weekend, and that was make his peace with Hannah. Seeing her again had resurrected all his feelings for her, and he couldn't imagine why he had let so much time pass without contacting her. Accordingly he stopped on the way home to buy some flowers, and, after he'd bathed and changed and before his courage could ebb, he ran down the flight of stairs that separated his flat from hers, and rang her bell.

The door opened at once, and from her welcoming smile he realised, with a sinking of the heart, that she'd been expecting someone else. She was wearing a lace dinner-dress in midnight blue and her hair was swept up on top of her head in a style he'd never seen before. It made her look at the same time stunningly beautiful and a stranger.

"Oh—David. Hello." Her eyes went uncertainly to the flowers held stiffly in his hand.

"Hello, Hannah. Have I called at a bad time?"

"You have, rather. I'm going out in a few minutes. In fact, I thought you were— But come in."

She stood to one side and he miserably stepped past her into the hallway. It had been redecorated since his last visit, emphasising both the time lapse and his sense of being out of place. But the sitting-room, with its windows open to the garden below, was blessedly familiar.

"Can I get you a drink?"

"Thanks." He held out the flowers.

"For the interpreting? That's sweet of you, but there's no need—I was glad to help. Is there any news?"

"No. But that's not why I brought the flowers." He paused, watching the delicate nape of her neck as she poured the drinks. Usually hidden by her hair, its fragile vulnerability constricted his throat.

"Oh?" She turned, handing him a glass.

"They're by way of a peace offering."

She half-smiled. "I thought diplomatic relations had been resumed."

"But not the relationship I *want* to resume, as you know damn well."

Her startled eyes went to his face. "David—"

"Yes, I'm sorry." He drew a deep breath. "I'd hoped we could talk, clear things up a bit."

"They're perfectly clear already."

The doorbell rang through the flat. They stood for a moment, unmoving. His eyes looked haunted, she thought. But it was a bit late, now, to make peace offerings, just because they'd met by chance and he'd been reminded of her existence.

"Excuse me," she said quietly, bending to put her glass down. He remained standing in a cocoon of misery, listening to the voices in the hall. Then she was back, flushed and talking too quickly.

"Charles, I don't think you've met David, from the flat upstairs. Charles Frobisher, David Webb."

"How do you do?" Frobisher smiled, held out his hand, and Webb forced himself to take it. The man oozed public-school confidence, from his accent, his clothes, his manner. He was wearing a dinner-jacket with black satin lapels. There was a carnation in his buttonhole, and Hannah was holding an exotic corsage. His own offering of spring flowers, still lying on the table, seemed vulgar by comparison.

Hannah, following his glance, said quickly, "I'll put these in water. They're lovely, David. Thank you so much."

She left the room and the two men stood awkwardly. At least Webb felt awkward. Frobisher seemed perfectly at home.

"We're going to a concert at the Mozart Rooms," he said easily. "Naomi Fairchild. Have you heard her play?"

"I'm afraid not."

Hannah came back with his flowers in a vase. She'd also pinned the orchid to her dress.

He emptied his glass quickly.

"I mustn't detain you. Thanks for the drink, Hannah. Have a good evening." He walked quickly from the room and let himself out of the flat. I've lost her, he thought numbly. And I've only myself to blame.

Nor was the Marshbanks' evening proceeding as smoothly as they'd wished. The Warwicks had arrived half an hour late, which caused problems to Claire's careful timing of the meal, and Beryl's eyes were red-rimmed. Her usual bright gaiety was nowhere in evidence, and Bernard sat like a zombie staring at his drink and making no response to Tom's conversational gambits.

When Claire went through to the kitchen, Beryl followed her, tears starting to her eyes. "Claire, I'm most awfully sorry. I don't know what's the matter with Bernard. He's hardly spoken since he came back at lunchtime, and he doesn't seem to hear when I speak to him."

Claire wished she could reassure her, but her own feelings towards Bernard were ambivalent at the moment. "Perhaps he's a lot on his mind," she offered.

"He—I shouldn't be telling you this, but I'd an awful job to get him here. He didn't seem to know what I was saying, and when I did get through to him, he said he couldn't come. I don't know what he meant; he hadn't any other engagements, and he wouldn't explain. He just kept repeating, 'I'm sorry, I can't go.' " She blew her nose and looked at Claire bleakly. "Do you think he's ill? He refused to let me phone the doctor. In fact, he—started shouting at me when I suggested it. It's not like Bernard at all."

"Perhaps he's worried about Arlette," Claire suggested, taking the prawn mousse out of the fridge. "He might feel it reflects on the university."

Beryl shook her head worriedly, her long nose red-tipped. "He's shutting me out, Claire. That's what frightens me."

"But surely Bernard's always self-contained? He strikes me as someone who prefers to solve his own problems, rather than discuss them with other people."

"But I'm not 'other people,' I'm his *wife!* I want to help him!" Her lips trembled. Claire slipped an arm round her and gave her a quick squeeze.

"Of course you do, and I'm sure he knows that. If it's anything serious, he'll tell you in his own good time. Now, be a love and help me carry these through, will you?"

As they reached the dining-room, she could hear Tom valiantly carrying on a monologue. Bernard's face had a shuttered look, like that of a blind man. He was staring down at the table and his gaze didn't refocus when the plate of mousse was set before him. For a moment, Claire wondered if he was going to ignore the entire meal. Then, to her relief, he picked up a fork—seemingly a reflex action—and began to eat.

She caught Beryl's eye and gave her a little nod of encouragement. Then, backing up Tom, she embarked on an anecdote about Katy. But beneath her surface chatter, her thoughts circled darkly round Bernard's strange behaviour. He'd always been odd, but not to this extent. Now, even Beryl was worried.

A thought suddenly came to her, so frightening that her stomach turned over, and, with a feeling of revulsion, she put down her fork. Suppose Bernard knew more than he was admitting? Suppose he was actually responsible for Arlette's disappearance? Was that why Mr. Webb was so interested in him?

CHAPTER 6

That evening, though Webb and the Marshbanks were too preoccupied to see it, an item about Arlette appeared in the television news bulletins, and the next morning the Sunday papers carried her photograph under the caption "Have you seen this woman?" The nation was becoming aware of her disappearance.

Having granted Jackson his requested day off, Webb drove alone to Steeple Bayliss, his easel and sketching equipment in the back of the car. The warm sunny weather was holding, and he planned to take at the very least an extended lunch hour, unless anything had blown up overnight.

But something had. Chris Ledbetter greeted him with a rueful grin. "Sorry, Dave, but we've really landed in it this time. We've got a psychic on our hands."

"A what?"

"I'm not sure what he calls himself—dowser, or something. He says he knows where Arlette is."

"Oh God!"

"And we can't fob him off, either. It seems he's wellknown and has had success in missing persons cases. The top brass says we have to—quote—'afford him every assistance'—unquote."

"That," said Webb feelingly, "is all we need."

"I'm just sorry to have to leave it to you."

"I can see it's breaking your heart."

Ledbetter grinned. "Tell you what, come and eat with us afterwards. Jackson not with you today?"

"No. The additions to the family are due, so he's staying close to home."

"I'll lend you Happy, then."

Which should also be a bundle of laughs, Webb thought gloomily. "Before I get out my Ouija board, what's the present state of play?"

"No stone, as they say, unturned. Did you see TV last night?" Webb shook his head. "Both BBC and ITV carried her photo and the press are running it today. For the rest, all the usual: picture in the *Police Gazette*, details on the computer, every police station alerted, Sally Army asked to keep a look-out, unidentified bodies checked."

"Any reported sightings?"

"They'll start coming in any minute. Only a couple to date, and they've been discounted."

"And our psychic friend knows where she is?"

"So he says. He saw the item on the news last night, and drove straight down from Yorkshire."

"Then what are we waiting for? Let him wrap up the case. Where is he?"

"Having breakfast in the canteen. I'll ring through and have him brought here as soon as he's finished."

Ed Barnsley looked like someone's favourite uncle. Marginally the right side of sixty, he had bushy eyebrows, rosy cheeks, and a beaming smile. Anyone less like a mystic Webb had never seen. His hand was taken in a warm, firm grasp.

"Right, lads, let's get down to work. I'll have the little lass back by dinnertime."

"You think she's still alive?" Webb asked. Despite his scepticism, the man's cheerful confidence lifted his spirits.

"Oh aye, no doubt of that. But she's frightened, poor lass. The sooner we get her out of there, the better."

"And where is she?" Ledbetter this time.

"Well, I'm not rightly sure. I've got the general direction, like, but if you'll give us an ordinance survey map, I'll narrow it down for you."

One was produced and spread on Ledbetter's desk. Barnsley took from his pocket a smooth round stone hanging from a piece of cord. While the two men watched, he held this above the map, letting it swing from its own momentum, and began a detailed quartering starting with the centre of Steeple Bayliss. Webb and Ledbetter avoided each other's eyes. For a while there was silence, punctuated only by Barnsley's heavy breathing. Then the stone jerked and began to circle in a clockwise direction, ever more quickly, until the man had to tighten his hold on the cord.

"Ah!" he said under his breath, and bent forward. Despite themselves, so did the policemen. Directly below the pendulum was the village of Popplewell, some six miles to the south-west.

Barnsley lowered his hand and the stone swung less widely until it pinpointed what looked to be a farm on the outskirts of the village. He closed his eyes.

"She's in a small, dark room—windows shuttered on the outside. There's a bed, a chair, and a washbasin in one corner. As far as I can see she's not tied up, but she's been knocked about a bit. There's a cut in her lip and a bruise on one cheek."

Webb said quietly, "How many people in the house?"

"Only one other, I reckon. A lad, tall, fair, about seventeen."

The description didn't fit anyone they'd interviewed. Webb said, "Do any of your men know the village, Inspector?"

"Jack Simpson comes from there."

"Is he in today?"

"Yes, he's working in the Incident Room." Ledbetter picked up the phone, and minutes later Simpson, a uniformed constable, was also bending over the map.

"I know the place, guv. Raintree Farm. It's been empty for the last year."

"Empty?" Barnsley, Webb, and Ledbetter spoke in unison, and Simpson looked at them in surprise.

"That's right. The land was sold off when old man Yardley died, but no one wanted the buildings. They're still owned by his son, but he's never been near the place, as far as I know."

"How old would the son be?"

"Oh, knocking on a bit. Fifties at least. The old man was in his eighties when he died."

So the son wasn't the tall fair youth. Webb gave himself a mental shake. He was acting as though he believed all this rubbish. Yet there was no denying either the dowser's sincerity or his supreme confidence. For all their sakes, Webb hoped he wouldn't be disappointed.

"What's the layout of the land, Constable?"

"It's pretty open, sir. Not a great deal of cover, if that's what you're thinking. A few spindly trees to the north, but there's a lane which leads only to the farm, and which could be watched from the windows."

"Are there any shutters?"

"I believe there are, come to think of it."

Despite himself, Webb's heartbeat quickened. "Let's hope they're all closed, then." He turned to Ledbetter and lowered his voice. "No need for the full stronghold routine. I suggest we take three cars in addition to mine; two officers in each. Mr. Barnsley thinks there's only one man, but there could be others around. Surprise is the main factor. If the girl is there, we want to avoid any hostage nonsense. I'll take Sergeant Hopkins with me, and I'd be glad of Constable Simpson too, if he can be spared from the Incident Room. Local knowledge is always helpful. Will you pick the others, Inspector? A bit of muscle mightn't go amiss."

Within twenty minutes they were driving past the university on the Oxbury road out of town. Webb was at the wheel of his own car, Happy Hopkins at his side, and Barnsley and Simpson in the back. It seemed a bizarre mission, and he'd have much preferred to have Jackson with him. He smiled inwardly, visualising the retelling of it to Ken. Heaven grant it had a happy ending.

After a few miles, a small road branched off to the right, signposted Popplewell. The village was sleeping peacefully in its Sunday lethargy. A straggle of cottages led towards the centre, formed traditionally by church, pub, post-office, and duck pond. As previously arranged, the four police cars parked there and the men got out. From the open church windows, the strains of "All Things Bright and Beautiful" reached them clearly. Simpson had advised them that Raintree Farm was at the far end of the village, and with a few curt words, Webb deployed his troops. Two men to circle widely to the right, two to the left, two to approach from behind. He, Hopkins, and Simpson would take the front.

"What about me?" asked Barnsley eagerly. "Happen I'll be needed, to pinpoint the room she's in."

Webb hesitated. "Very well. Provided you obey orders implicitly. We don't like involving members of the public in operations like this."

As Simpson had said, the lane leading to the farm was in full view of the house windows, but they were indeed shuttered. That confirmation of Barnsley's information gave Webb an illogical sense of hope. Simpson had changed from his uniform jacket before leaving the station, borrowing a cream-coloured blazer. There was nothing to proclaim to any watcher that the police were approaching.

But no watcher was apparent. The farmhouse stared blindly out at them with no visible sign of life. As they reached it, they could see men to either side closing in simultaneously. Webb waited several tense minutes before receiving confirmation that the windows all round the house were shuttered. There was no way to make a silent entry. He gave a signal and two of the heaviest men put their shoulders to the door. Surprisingly, it gave at the first assault. The six of them moved in a body into the dim, musty-smelling building. A scuffling came from the room to the right.

"In there!" Webb snapped, and flung open the door. He found himself staring at the terrified face of a young man. A camp bed had been erected near the window, where cracks of light filtered through the shutters. On the floor beside it was a mug half full of tea, a milk bottle, cigarettes. A paperback lay face down on the bed.

"Where is she?" Webb demanded. The youth jerked his head upwards. "Search him," he commanded, turned, and with Barnsley close behind him, clattered up the bare boards of the staircase.

"Back room," panted Barnsley. "There!"

The door he pointed at had a large iron key in the lock. An amateur jailer. Webb turned it and flung open the door. Across the room a girl cowered on the bare ticking of a mattress, staring at them with wide, frightened eyes. There was a cut in her lip and a bruise on her left cheek. Webb hadn't the slightest idea who she was. But she wasn't Arlette Picard.

At Melbray, the Art Appreciation course was in its second and final day. All seemed to be going smoothly. Mid-morning coffee had been served, and the kitchens had lunch underway. Claire stretched, looking longingly at the sunlit gardens outside the window. Daphne Farlow, who was on duty with her, looked up.

"I say, it's rotten about that girl going missing, isn't it?"

Claire sighed. The last thing she wanted to talk about was Arlette. "Yes," she said.

But Daphne was not to be put off. "I saw her parents arriving at the station. Prof Warwick was with them, and two other bods." Daphne hesitated and glanced at Beryl's empty desk. She was not on duty today, and after the previous evening's dinner-party, Claire was relieved. Not that she felt up to coping with Daphne, either. Daphne Farlow, at forty-five, still looked and spoke like an over-grown schoolgirl. She wore her dark hair caught back with a rubberband and hanging in a straight ponytail down her back. She was earnest, gauche, and wellmeaning, given to shrieks of laughter when mildly amused. Yet Claire liked her. There was something innocent and therefore vulnerable about her which aroused Claire's protective instincts. She found herself trying to shield Daphne from the harsher aspects of modern-day living, which, as she confessed to herself, was ridiculous.

"Did Prof Warwick mention them last night?" Daphne was asking.

Claire frowned. "Last night?"

"You said they were coming to dinner. Beryl and her husband."

"Yes, they did." Claire spoke shortly, surprised at Daphne's persistence.

"I thought they might know the Froggies. Old pals, or something?"

"Daphne, what is this? How could the Warwicks possibly know Arlette's parents? They've only just arrived in the country."

"I know, but—" Daphne looked up, her face flooding with miserable colour. "You see, I saw them. This morning. And they certainly looked pretty friendly."

Claire stared at her. "Who did you see this morning?"

"Prof Warwick and Madame. They were in that little coffee shop in Lazenby Road. It was a fluke that I saw them—I'd just popped in to get some doughnuts. They were over in a corner, leaning towards each other and talking very intently—in French, I think, though I couldn't really hear. And—and he was holding both her hands," she finished in a rush.

Claire felt slightly sick. "Professor Warwick and Madame Picard?"

Daphne nodded. "I feel rotten, spilling the beans like this, but you're Beryl's chum and I thought you should know. Of course, I'd rather *die* than breathe a word to her."

Claire moistened her lips. "Let's get this quite straight. You're sure you couldn't be mistaken? If they were in a dark corner, and you'd come in from bright sunshine—?"

Daphne shook her head emphatically. "It was them all right. No question about it."

"Did he see you?"

"Lord no, he never took his eyes off her. And he'd chosen a pretty out-of-the-way place; he wouldn't expect anyone he knew to be there."

"But you were," Claire said flatly.

"Yes. I take a short cut that way to avoid the traffic lights, but I've never been in the café before. It was jolly hard luck on him, wasn't it? I mean, if he—" She floundered, but Claire was incapable of helping her. "Gosh, Claire, I hope I've done the right thing, telling you about it."

"Yes, of course." But what on earth could it mean? *Bernard,* of all people. And what chance had they had, to know each other well enough to meet in an obscure café and hold hands? Daphne *must* be mistaken.

But her comforting conclusion was weighed against Bernard's agitation the previous evening, his immobility in the garden in the small hours. *Something* had thrown him seriously off-balance. Could it be Madame Picard? Yet if the Warwicks *had* known her, Beryl would have said, surely. Unless Beryl didn't know? With a sinking heart, Claire admitted the possibility that there might be several things Beryl didn't know.

She felt a flash of anger. Daphne had no right to discover Bernard's secret and then, by confiding in her, hand over the responsibility for it.

Daphne, watching her silent deliberations with some anxiety, offered a less than tactful olive branch.

"I say, would you like a doughnut?"

"No," Claire snapped, "I most definitely would not."

CHAPTER 7

Barnsley was at the same time triumphant and chastened. "Well, I knew *some* lass was there. It came to me the minute I heard 'Broadshire' on the telly. But I'm sorry it weren't the one you want."

"Never mind," Dave told him. "We're glad to have this one back safe." They knew by now that the shivering, bruised sixteen-year-old was Debbie Lester, who had run away after a row with her mother. Her abductor attended the same school. He'd offered to help, and she'd trustingly gone with him. "You haven't any other vibes, have you?" Webb added hopefully. The vindication of the man had shaken him, even if he'd got the identity wrong.

"Can't say I have. I'm right sorry, Chief Inspector." The man looked crestfallen.

Dave shrugged and gave him a rueful grin. "I thought it was too good to be true."

So that was that. Furthermore, Chris had had to withdraw his lunch invitation. "Sorry, Dave, another time; Happy and I'll be tied up all day now. But this is our pigeon. There's nothing to keep you, surely, now that you've made your report? Why not take the afternoon off and come back fresh tomorrow?"

"I might, at that," Dave conceded. "I did put my sketching gear in the car, in case chance offered."

"Excellent. Happy sketching, then!"

Webb went to *The Barley Mow* for a late lunch. The boat was crowded with Sunday drinkers, leaning over the deck rail and thronging the dark interior.

Shouldering his way to the bar, he ordered the pastie he'd enjoyed on his last visit.

"Sorry, mate," the barman told him, "only cold on Sundays."

"Fair enough. Pork pie and salad, then." Looking about him, he saw one or two faces he recognised, but no one seemed anxious to meet his eye. Perhaps talking with a copper spoiled the taste of the beer. Well, it was no skin off his nose.

The pie was good; crisp pastry, and succulent jellied meat within. What was Hannah doing now? The thought came before he could stop it. Perhaps roasting beef for her fancy man. The bitter phrase didn't ease his pain. She'd said she'd never marry; would she change her mind if Charles Bloody Frobisher popped the question? Who the hell was he, anyway? Webb stabbed viciously at the tomato on his plate.

Still, he didn't want to marry her himself. Once bitten, very definitely twice shy on that score, specially after Susan's brief comeback. So what was he moaning about? It was just that their relationship had been so perfect, each content with the limitations mutually set. Until he'd blotted his copybook over Susan. Come to think of it, what was *she* doing now? He hadn't seen her since the morning after she'd spent the night at his flat, when, as they came downstairs together, Hannah had opened her door to take in the milk. (He'd not seen Hannah since, either, till last Friday, and that was much less understandable.) But he'd heard soon after that Susan had left Shillingham. Did he drive her away? "You don't own the bloody town!" she'd flung at him. Perhaps she'd decided that he did, after all.

He sighed, pushing the remainder of his salad to one side and finishing his beer. To hell with the lot of them. He'd have a perfect afternoon all to himself in the glorious countryside, and he was willing to bet he'd feel much the better for it.

He drove north out of town, leaving the main road just short of the Gloucestershire border and winding his way through undulating countryside in search of a good place to stop. After a while he parked the car, collected his equipment, and set off over the flower-filled meadows, climbing steadily as he went. Another month, and the poppies would be out. Every year he did a couple of watercolours of them. They were his favourite wild flower. He smiled, remembering Mrs. Marshbanks' interest in his paintings, but he wouldn't show them to her. He regarded them as a means of self-expression, and therefore private to himself.

He paused and surveyed his surroundings. This would do. There wasn't a building in sight, even from this altitude. He must be a good ten miles from Steeple Bayliss.

But having set up his easel, he decided to take a nap first. He'd not slept well the last couple of nights, worries about the case and thoughts of Hannah keeping his brain overactive. Now, his lunchtime beer combined with the warm sunshine to make him pleasantly drowsy.

He took off his sweater, rolled it into a pillow, and lay down on the warm, prickly grass. In the distance a sheep bleated plaintively, answered by one nearer at hand. His nostrils were filled with the sweet, hay-like scent of dry grass and his closed eyelids presented a changing palette of vibrant colours.

If only the girl they'd found that morning had been Arlette. He'd immersed himself so deeply in her over the last four days that he felt he knew her better than many of her acquaintances: knew her as a vibrant, attractive girl, fun-loving, flirtatious perhaps, but, in Simon's opinion at least, not promiscuous. Where in heaven's name was she? He was becoming steadily more fearful for her. He frowned at the thought, settled his head more comfortably on the sweater, and slept.

It was late afternoon when Claire arrived home from Melbray. Tom was out playing golf. A pity; she wanted to tell him Daphne's story. She made herself a cup of tea and drank it walking restlessly about the kitchen, her thoughts revolving round the tensions of the dinner-party.

Surely things weren't seriously wrong between the Warwicks? Beryl gave the impression they were devoted to each other, and Bernard was so calm, so unchanging, so predictable, that it was impossible to imagine him showing any kind of emotion. Yet it was precisely because he was always in control that his evident loss of it had been so disturbing.

What had caused that dissociation? Madame Picard? The whole idea was preposterous. She went over again what Daphne had told her, unable to latch onto any facet that she could accept. Would a distraught mother, newly arrived in the country, even temporarily desert her husband to sit in some out-of-the-way café holding hands with a man she'd just met? Illogically, what Claire found hardest to believe was that Bernard—*Bernard*—would hold hands with anyone, anywhere.

Had anyone else recounted the story, Claire might have suspected sheer, mendacious troublemaking. But Daphne was so guileless, so transparently upset by what she'd seen, that against all her instincts, Claire had no option but to believe her. Or at least, to believe that was what she *thought* she'd seen.

Claire set her cup down with a positive little thump. She'd go round and see Beryl. That would put her mind at rest. She'd probably find the pair of them in the back garden, and then she could laugh at her imaginings.

But her optimism faded when the front door opened. Beryl's face was red-eyed and grim. She stood silently to one side and Claire stepped past her into the panelled hall.

"Come into the kitchen," Beryl said. "I'm doing the sandwiches for tea."

"Where's Bernard?" Claire asked brightly, following her. "Out in the garden?"

Beryl didn't reply, and when she turned her mouth was trembling. "I don't know," she said eventually, "and that's the least of the things I don't know about Bernard." Mechanically she picked up the knife and went on buttering the bread.

Claire said gently, "What's wrong, Beryl?"

"What's wrong," Beryl repeated deliberately, laying pieces of ham on the bread with exaggerated care, "is that I've suddenly realised not only that Bernard doesn't love me, but that he never has."

"Oh, Beryl, no! That can't be right! You've been so happy together. Surely this is just—"

"I doubt if Bernard's been happy. I have, because I've been fooling myself. I've spent the last ten years trying to please him, and all the time he scarcely knew I was there."

"But what makes you think that? If it's just that you've had a row—"

"A row!" Beryl gave a choking laugh. "That's one word for it. I thought he was going to kill me!"

"Beryl!"

"I wanted to help him, you see. But he turned on me in a blind white fury, ranting and raving about the 'wasted years.' I didn't understand half what he was saying, but what *did* come through was that he could scarcely bear me near him." She was crying openly now, sobbing little hiccups punctuating her words, her plain face totally defenceless and ugly with her grief. Claire put a tentative hand on her arm, and was shaken off.

"I don't want your sympathy! God, you're so *smug*, Claire! What do you know about it, mouthing platitudes like of course it will be all right? It won't, and it never has been, all right, though I didn't realise till now. It's over, totally and completely finished. If I can accept it, surely you can."

"But—but why?" Claire stammered, trying to modify her rôle as comforter. "Why now, all of a sudden?"

"Because quite suddenly he can't take any more. And neither can I!" And as Claire watched, dumbfounded, Beryl caught up the breadknife and started plunging it again and again into the loaf on the table, finally collapsing over it in a paroxysm of weeping.

The sound of a car horn woke Webb and he blinked, looking at his watch. Five o'clock. He must have slept for a couple of hours. So much for an afternoon's sketching. Chris would pull his leg tomorrow. It wasn't too late, though the light wasn't as good as it had been. He sat up, rubbing a hand across his face, and remembered what woke him. He must be nearer a road than he'd thought.

He got to his feet, brushing the blades of grass off shirt and trousers and shaking out the rolled-up sweater. The sun had left the area and it was noticeably cooler. He put his sweater on, grateful for its crumpled warmth.

Should he make a start on some work, or go home for a cup of tea? Without the sun, the stretch of rolling countryside had a desolate look, and despite the sweater he shivered. The tea won, hands down. He'd come and sketch another day. Again, over the brow of the hill behind him, came the impatient blast of a horn. Curious, he walked up the slope and found himself on a ridge which dropped away in front of him to the valley floor some hundred feet below. Along that floor stretched what looked like a busy highway. At a guess it would be the Nailsworth to Shillingham road. He stood for a moment watching the cars rushing towards and past each other. There was a strong breeze here on the exposed hilltop, and Webb sneezed suddenly, fumbling in his pocket for a handkerchief. But the wind caught it, tugged it out of his hand, and floated it over the edge.

Swearing, he bent cautiously forward, and his sudden coldness had nothing to do with the wind. The heap of camel and blue huddled on the ledge some fifty feet below was identification enough, without the poignant confirmation of the scrap of fuchsia silk fluttering bravely on a gorse bush. He had found Arlette.

With no hope inside him, he made his way backwards down the uneven hillside, fingers scrabbling for a hold as his feet dislodged miniature landslides of pebbles and tufts of grass. There was no way she could be alive, not with her head at that angle. Twelve feet above the ledge he stopped, the stench reaching his nostrils making him gag. Five days in the warm weather had turned a pretty, laughing girl into something foul. He forced himself to look down. She was lying like a discarded doll, her pretty hair tangled in the gorse bush which had arrested her fall. The heel of one sandal had broken and was hanging by a thread to the shoe.

His first reaction was a helpless anger. All that life and vitality, drained away into the rocky hillside. What a waste—what a diabolical waste. Then he thought of the polite, frantic couple who were her parents. With a deep sigh, he started to make his way back up the hill.

She was feeling calmer now, and not a little ashamed of her outburst in front of Claire. She'd go round tomorrow and apologise. In fact, what she was most conscious of was a feeling of anticlimax. Because an hour after Claire left, Bernard had come home and, apart from that glazed look in his eyes, had behaved no differently from usual. Which is to say he went out to water the plants and trim the edges of the lawn as if nothing had happened.

They had their usual Sunday tea—the ham sandwiches which had witnessed so much drama in their making, and a cake she'd baked the previous day, before the storm broke. She thought back to that different self who had made it, happy to be trying out a new recipe, looking forward to the dinner-party that evening, awaiting Bernard's return for lunch. The self who had foolishly imagined herself loved, or at any rate the object of some affection.

She bit her lip as she recalled the words he'd thrown at her, each of them hooked to dig painfully into her memory and cling on there. How could he have lived with her for ten years, without giving an inkling of his true feelings? If they *were* his true feelings. Perhaps he was suffering from a mental illness, a kind of brain storm? Perhaps he hadn't meant those things after all, didn't even realise he'd said them? Because this evening he'd been as calm and polite as usual, with no hint of that white-faced fury which had terrified her.

Now they were sitting as they always did, she with some embroidery and Bernard with his papers. But he wasn't reading them; she could tell. He spent a lot of time staring out of the window at the darkening garden. Every now and then he'd give a little start, force his eyes back to the papers, and turn one over. But his mind was elsewhere. What was he thinking about?

Cécile, Cécile. He could hardly believe she'd come back. All those years of longing, withering away without her, and now she was here. The husband was of no consequence, a weakling, lying in a darkened room ever since their arrival and of no comfort to her. A migraine, for God's sake! It was a woman's complaint, but in her sweetness and loyalty she made excuses for him. Bernard didn't dispute them; he could afford to be generous, because it was himself she loved. He was convinced of it. Not that she'd said so in as many words. She was too distraught about the girl to think clearly, and he appreciated that. But subconsciously, desperate for the support and comfort her husband couldn't give, she had turned to him. Which was as it should be.

The snip of Beryl's embroidery scissors broke into his reverie. He blinked, looked down again at the papers in his lap. Beryl. There'd been a scene at lunchtime, when he'd returned from his meeting with Cécile. He'd said too much, he knew, though he couldn't remember what. Poor, plain Beryl, with her colourless eyebrows and her spinsterish ways. He recalled his earlier fantasy, of murdering her because she loved him. Now, it was in the bounds of possibility, though he hoped it wouldn't come to that. After all, she'd had ten happy years; Gaston three times as many with Cécile. In all fairness, they should now be prepared to step down.

But nothing definite could be said until the girl was found. He frowned, trying to visualise her, but she'd made no impression on him; he'd no memory of her unique to himself, only the picture he'd seen in the paper. He felt doubly cheated, by that lack of personal memory and by not having known who she was. But she didn't resemble her mother. If she'd had Cécile's large brown eyes, her smoothly dark hair—

He clenched his fists, feeling himself tremble. God, how he wanted her! He was fifty years old, but the only fulfilment he had known had been at twenty, with her. It wasn't too late. Now he could *live* again, with his beloved. His beloved.

"Shall I put the news on, dear?"

He jumped and frowned. "I beg your pardon?"

"The news. It's time, if you'd like to see it."

"Very well." Why must she interrupt? Cécile—

Beryl said on a high note, "Oh, Bernard! God, no!"

Odd. There on the screen was the picture he'd just conjured up of Arlette. *What* were they saying? Dead? Oh, my love! My poor, poor sweet—

The announcer's voice droned on. There were pictures of a steep bank over a busy road, and some activity half way up the slope—men moving around and a plastic tent being erected. Had he missed something? Had she been *murdered?* If someone had killed Cécile's daughter, he, Bernard, would personally strangle him with his bare hands.

That fellow Webb's face filled the screen. So the police were treating her death as suspicious. Now perhaps they'd get on with finding her killer, instead of pestering him.

"Her poor parents," Beryl said softly, as the news item changed. "How must they be feeling?"

He should go to her, he thought in agitation. No doubt Gaston was prostrate on his sick-bed. She needed his own strength, the force of his love, to carry her through.

In a flash of clarity, he saw the purpose in it. It was necessary for her to suffer, and for Gaston's inadequacy to be revealed. Only then would she realise that she'd never stopped loving himself.

"It's fate, you see," he said aloud.

Beryl looked startled. "What is?"

"The girl's death." He shouldn't need to explain. Couldn't she understand anything?

"Whatever do you mean?" She was staring at him wide-eyed, and to his annoyance there was that look of fear that he'd noticed at lunchtime.

"It's plain enough, surely," he said with heavy patience. "It's the only way to—" He broke off. What was he saying? He really must be careful about thinking aloud. Who knew what he might say? Might already have said?

"The only way to what?" There was a quaver in Beryl's voice.

"Never mind. Nothing. You wouldn't understand."

"Bernard, dear, I don't think you're well. Won't you go and see the doctor? To please me? I'm sure there's something he—"

"There's nothing wrong with me, Beryl, that can't be put right quite simply."

She tried to smile. "Well, that's good news."

"I hope you continue to think so," he said.

"Simon?" It was Iris's voice, and she sounded as though she'd been crying.

"Hello, Iris." He was in a state of shock himself. If he hadn't arranged to meet Arlette, if she'd done something entirely different with her day, would she still be alive? It didn't bear thinking about. His memory of her was so vivid, the colours of it so strong and undiminished, that his brain wouldn't accept she was dead.

"Are you there, Simon?"

"Sorry. Yes."

"I've—I've just seen it on TV."

"I know. I feel awful, too."

"It isn't only that, though. Was she murdered, do you think?"

"It's too soon to say."

"They said on the news there were suspicious circumstances, so I—"

His voice sharpened. "What is it, Iris? Is there something you haven't told us?"

"She made me promise not to—swore me to secrecy."

"Arlette did?"

"Yes. She said if I ever breathed a word—"

"For God's sake, Iris! What is it?"

"Someone she used to meet. That no one knew about."

"Who?"

Iris gave a little sob. "If I'd told you before, would it have stopped her being killed?"

"How do I know until you tell me?" He stopped, having pity on the weeping girl. "I don't think so. It looks as though she died the day she disappeared."

"Oh." She gave a relieved little hiccup.

"Well, come on. Who was she meeting?"

"I don't know if she met him on Tuesday," Iris said cautiously.

"*Who was it?*"

"Mr. Morgan. William and Olga's father, who she gave coaching to."

Simon let out his breath. "Was she seeing him regularly?"

"He brought her home every week. Only they didn't come straight home. I was up in my room once, drawing the curtains. It was dark, so it must have been March sometime. And I saw her get out of a car just down the road. A man got out too, and gave her a long kiss. I asked her about it after, and that's when she told me."

"Thanks, Iris. For letting me know."

"Will I get into trouble for not saying? A policeman came asking questions, but I didn't tell him, because I'd promised not to."

"Never mind. We'll follow it up now."

"Mr. Morgan won't know it was me who told you?"

"No, I promise. Don't worry."

Reassured that she had done her duty, albeit belatedly, Iris put down the phone.

It was ten o'clock, and Webb had gone back to Ledbetter's house after all, too weary to resist his pressing invitation. Arlette's body had been extensively photographed, examined by the police surgeon, the pathologist, and the Scene of Crime officers, and finally wrapped in plastic and manoeuvred down the hill to the waiting hearse. Webb himself had accompanied it to the morgue. There, she'd been identified by her parents, and a post-mortem was arranged for the following morning. Now, sitting in the Ledbetters' pleasant sitting-room, the two men were relaxing at last.

"We'll soon know if she was dead when she went over the edge," Chris Ledbetter was saying. He was sitting in the corner of the sofa, his injured leg laid along it, and, the snack supper finished, a rare glass of brandy in his hand.

Webb took a sip from his own glass. "There was no other obvious cause. But if she died from the fall, *did* she fall, or was she pushed? Because what in hell was she doing way out there, when she was expecting to catch the one-whatever to Shillingham? She was hardly dressed for walking, in those sandals."

Janet Ledbetter came into the room, followed by her daughter carrying a fresh pot of coffee. Emma at seventeen was ravishing. Lucky she took after her father, Webb thought affectionately, for though he was fond of Janet, no one could call her goodlooking. She had soft, mousy-coloured hair, a small, pinched face, and a shy smile. An odd choice, perhaps, for someone as flamboyantly handsome as Chris. Cynics suggested he'd married her to avoid competition, but Webb knew that was untrue. Not only was Chris entirely lacking in vanity, but the Ledbetters were one of the happiest couples he knew, and he envied them for it.

"You'll stay the night, of course, David," Janet said matter-of-factly, pouring the coffee.

"Oh no, I—" Webb began. Then stopped. The thought of the fifty-minute drive through the dark countryside was not inviting, and he was bone tired, despite his hillside sleep. "Well, if you're sure it's no trouble," he ended lamely.

"None whatever. The bed's been aired all week, in the hope you might stop over."

"That's good of you. In that case, may I give Ken Jackson a ring?"

Jackson's voice vibrated down the wire. "Where are you, guv? I've been trying to get you ever since the news broke. Too bad about the girl."

"Yes. I'm still at SB, Ken—staying over with DI Ledbetter. Have a look on my desk in the morning, and bring over anything of interest."

"Will do." Jackson paused, then his voice quickened. "I've some news myself, and all—good news, this time. The twins made their appearance at three o'clock. How about that? Spot on time, clever little blighters!"

"That's great, Ken! Congratulations! Millie OK?"

"Fine, now, and pleased as punch. Boy and girl again, so we're still even-stevens. Tessa and Tim, we're calling them. Guv—it's hardly the time to ask, but Millie made me promise. How would you feel about being Tim's godfather?"

Webb's eyes bored into the patterned wallpaper, a welter of emotions buffeting him. He said quietly, "I should be honoured, Ken. Thank you."

"That's great! We'll give him David as his second name. Millie'll be so pleased."

"Give her my love—and I'll see you in the morning." Webb put the phone down and stood for a moment with his hand resting on it before he turned back to the room. His thoughts were a jumble and too philosophical for comfort. One girl dies, another is born. Something like that. But he was more touched than he cared to admit by the Jacksons' request.

"Do I gather the baby's arrived?" Ledbetter asked, as he went back to his chair.

"Both of them! A boy and a girl." He raised his glass. "So let's drink to them—to Tessa, and to Timothy David, my godson!"

CHAPTER 8

Jackson said, "I've a message for you from Simon. The landlady's daughter's been on again. Says she saw Morgan and Arlette necking when he took her home."

"Ah! I thought those hooded eyes concealed something. But why the hell didn't she tell you?"

"She'd promised Arlette." Jackson grinned as Webb raised his eyes to the heavens. "Come on, guv, you were young once. Remember when promises meant something?"

"Spare me the philosophy, Ken. We'd better get onto the bowls club he talked about. Check what time he gets there on Mondays and how long he stays. Then phone his wife and find out where he works. We'll call round as soon as the PM's finished. I'm on my way there now."

"Hope your breakfast stays down!"

"So do I."

Jackson joined Happy Hopkins in the main office. "I must say," grumbled the Steeple Bayliss sergeant, "your governor has a strange way of relaxing. Does he often find bodies on his afternoon off?"

"Makes a habit of it," Jackson answered with a grin. "The old principle of think of something else and you'll find what you're looking for."

Hopkins grunted. "You heard we had a weirdo with us yesterday?"

"No? What kind of weirdo?"

"Oh, a real screwball. Insisted he knew where the girl was —said she was holed up in a farmhouse at Popplewell. According to HQ he'd a good record, so we had to go chasing off with him—me and your governor and half a dozen of the boys."

"Get away! Well, at least it'd give you a laugh."

"Except," said Happy morosely, "that the laugh was on us. There *was* a girl there right enough—the other one we've been looking for."

"You mean he was right? She was at the place he said?"

"Yep. He described the house to a T, and the room where she was—even that she'd a bruise on her face. Make you sick, wouldn't it? We look for one girl for ten days, and a nutcase finds her for us. Then your governor stumbles over the other on his afternoon off. I reckon I'm wasting my time here."

"But *how* did he know? Did he explain?"

"Swung a stone over a map, the DI said. Gives me the willies to think about it. Anyway, my lad, you were well out of it, believe me. What did you get up to on your free day? Trip over any bodies?"

"No, I became a father again. Twice over."

"Well, congratulations and all that, but rather you than me. Think of it—double the nappies and double the burps! I've three kids myself, but at least we had them one at a time!"

The post-mortem, as Webb had suspected, showed that Arlette died as a result of her fall, and most probably on the day she disappeared. Their first priority, therefore, was to discover who she was on her way to meet when she saw Peter Campbell. Nigel Morgan was as good a place as any to start. Jackson had learned he was a partner in a firm of estate agents, with premises down on Riverside over-looking the water.

After the sunshine of the last week, the weather was cooler and dull, and the River Darrant gleamed like metal under the grey sky. Morgan was expecting them, and led them through the front office festooned with photographs of desirable properties, to his private room at the back. His skin had an unhealthy sheen and he was smoking in quick, nervous puffs.

"I don't mind telling you, Chief Inspector, it's been a great shock to us," he said, before Webb could speak. "The children in particular are most upset. I mean, she was with us as usual on the Monday, and then, the next day—" He stopped, took out a handkerchief, and wiped his forehead. "Do you know how it happened?"

"Her neck was broken," Webb said baldly.

"Poor girl. What a tragic accident."

"If it *was* an accident. We have to discover how and why she went out there, and whether she was alone when she fell."

Morgan stared at him, his eyes dilating. "You're not suggesting somebody *killed* her?"

"We're treating it with suspicion till we learn different. Now, Mr. Morgan, I don't think you've been quite honest with us. You knew Arlette better than you led us to believe, isn't that so?"

Morgan stared at him for a moment. Then he put his head in his hands. The cigarette, jammed between his fingers, released its tenuous spiral to coil about his head like a smoky halo.

"For a start," Webb went on when he didn't speak, "you left home on Mondays at 8 P.M., to run Arlette home. Yet you never arrived at the bowls club before nine. Can you explain that?"

"I didn't say I went straight there."

"But nor did you take Miss Picard straight home."

"Maybe not, but there's nothing sinister about it. We went for something to eat."

Webb was taken aback. "Something to eat?"

"That's right. The Kings have their meal at seven, which meant by the time Arlette got home, her supper'd dried up in the oven. So we started dropping in somewhere on the way back."

"Where did you take her?"

"Oh, round and about."

"Where you wouldn't meet anyone you knew?"

Morgan flushed. "She enjoyed Chinese food, so we tried different restaurants on the outskirts of town. I didn't eat myself—my wife and I had our meal during the coaching session—but I'd have a glass of wine and some coffee. And we'd talk. To be frank, I found her fascinating. She was so young and full of enthusiasm, it was a tonic just being with her. There really was no harm in it."

"But it didn't stay that innocent, did it?" Webb said implacably.

Morgan straightened. "What the devil do you mean?"

"Mr. Morgan, you were seen embracing the girl."

"By whom?" He was still blustering, but there was panic in his eyes.

"Does it matter? You don't deny it, do you?"

"I might have kissed her goodnight. It meant no more than shaking hands."

Webb raised an eyebrow, making no direct reply. "Did you see her on Tuesday morning?"

"No, of course I didn't. My God, you don't think *I* pushed her over?"

"Where were you on Tuesday, between ten-thirty and two o'clock?"

"Here, of course."

"All the time?"

"As far as I remember." He pulled a desk diary towards him, and Webb saw that his hand was shaking. "Oh yes, I did slip out for a while, to inspect a couple of houses."

"At what time?"

"One at ten-thirty, the other an hour later. Then I went to lunch, and was back here at two."

"Where were these houses?"

"The first was in Pemberton Crescent and the other in Larchfield Road. They were both fairly large, so I allowed plenty of time."

"The name of the owners?"

Morgan told him, and Jackson noted them down.

"Were you having an affair with Miss Picard, Mr. Morgan?"

A dull flush stained the man's face and neck. "No, I was not."

"You weren't frank with us before, sir. It would be as well if you were this time."

"Damn you, I was *not.* The odd kiss and cuddle, yes, but nothing more."

"When was the last time you saw her?"

"Monday night, as I told you. We went to the Willow Gardens and I ran her home afterwards. Which reminds me, have you finished with the car yet? I'm having to borrow my wife's and it's most inconvenient."

"We'll get it back to you as soon as we can."

"So where does that leave us?" Jackson asked, as they walked back to their car.

"God knows. He's a shifty-looking bloke, for all his posh accent. I sure as hell wouldn't buy any houses from him. He *could* have pushed her over—in a fit of frustration, say, if she wouldn't play ball. Check with the house owners that he called at the times he said." Webb ran a hand frustratedly through his hair. "The devil of it is, if she was killed simply by being pushed over the edge, it wouldn't have needed much strength. A girl could have done it."

"Specially if she was jealous, like they said in the pub?"

"It's a possibility. Jane, wasn't it? 'I thought she'd kill Arlette when she went off with Mike.' Perhaps she did, Ken. Add her name to the list, and the gang Arlette went round with. Happy's already interviewed them, but with a possible murder on our hands, we'll have to follow it up. And there are still two more lecturers to see, Baker and Lennard. As soon as the inquest's over, we'll get back up there."

They spent a routine and unproductive afternoon interviewing for themselves the tutors and post-graduates who had been Arlette's friends. Mike, Steve, Alan, and Charlie, whose names had figured in several statements, were not the offhand, unconcerned group Hopkins had depicted, but, faced with Arlette's death, subdued and anxious to help. The young lecturers, too, regretted their previous attitude.

"I was pretty fed up with her," Philip Baker admitted. "I thought she was playing hooky. She'd supposedly had some upset the previous week, which meant reshuffling her classes, and this time she'd not even bothered to phone. But I never dreamt she'd come to any harm."

No, neither he nor Mark Lennard had known her well.

"Ever seen her in the company of other tutors or lecturers?"

"Only in the bar or the departmental coffee-room."

They could be lying, but Webb didn't think so. "I hear she caused some jealousy up here. Any girl you can think of who might have had it in for her?"

Mark Lennard stared at him in horror. "Not to the extent of killing her. Surely you don't think that?"

"At the moment we don't know that anyone killed her, Dr. Lennard. But if they did, it could have been on the spur of the moment, and regretted immediately afterwards. We wouldn't necessarily be looking for a hardened criminal."

But the two men weren't prepared to give any names which might be considered suspect. Which left 'Jane,' and having declared his interest, Webb felt it wise to elicit her surname elsewhere.

By the time they'd done so it was after five-thirty, and they found her in the bar. She was a pert twenty-three-year-old in shirt and jeans, perched on a stool and, unlike the men, neither apologetic nor beset with guilt. There were several other people about, but she declined Webb's offer to go somewhere private.

"Nothing to hide, have I?" she said defiantly.

Webb tried to ignore his interested audience. "I hear you weren't too friendly with Arlette Picard?"

"Can you blame me? Went off with my fella, didn't she?"

Jane answered frankly. "Naturally I wasn't chuffed. Who would be? Doesn't mean I pushed her off any cliff, though. Did someone think I might have? What bloody cheek!"

"Who was your—er—fellow?" Webb inquired.

"Mike Partridge. I know him from home and we've been going out since we were sixteen, which made it worse."

Partridge hadn't mentioned Jane. "And Arlette went round with him?"

"Only till she'd got him hooked, then he became just one of her gang. And I'm damn sure he didn't get what he was after—that wasn't how she played it. Jam tomorrow but never jam today. Bloody serves him right."

"Did any of the other girls feel as you do?"

"God, yes. We'd have a right moan over our cocoa. But it wasn't *serious*, copper. I mean, OK, we'd have liked to see her taken down a peg, but not this way."

Which was how they had to leave it.

Claire pushed open the gate of her daughter's house and glanced into the pram in the garden. It was empty. Sarah came to the door, the baby under one arm.

"Hello, Mum. Come in. I'm just getting Katy's tea."

Claire circumvented the packing cases in the tiny hall. "Are you beginning to get sorted out?"

Sarah laughed. "Not so that you'd notice. The dining-room's still full of junk, and Paul can't get the car in the garage. Have you time for a cuppa?"

"I'd love one. Let me take Katy while you get it." She sat down at the kitchen table, her granddaughter on her knee. "I only came for a chat, really. I've been feeling so depressed all day."

"I know." Sarah sobered. "Have you spoken to Sy?"

"Only briefly. He's pretty shaken, poor lamb."

"Who wouldn't be? Beryl sounded upset, too."

"Beryl?" Claire spoke more sharply than she'd intended. "You've been speaking to Beryl?"

Sarah turned in surprise, kettle in hand. "Yes; we've been

asked out for a meal on Friday, and I know it's your theatre night. So, since she'd offered to babysit, I took her up on it. Why?"

"Oh—nothing." Claire smoothed Katy's silky hair and gave her an impulsive hug. The memory of Beryl repeatedly plunging the knife into the loaf was not a comfortable one, but she was probably being silly. Anyway, Beryl had come round this morning to apologise. "I think she's under a strain," she added in mitigation.

"Really? She seemed fine on Tuesday. Gosh, Mum, I've just thought. While we were all at home having tea, Arlette was—" She broke off with a shaky little laugh. "Sorry! You came round to be cheered up!"

But Claire followed her line of thought. "Simon phoned, remember, while you were there?"

"And I called her a *femme fatale.* So she was, but in a different sense." She shivered. "I hope they find out what happened."

"Mr. Webb came to see us. You remember Simon speaking of him?"

"Why?" Sarah's voice was sharp. "What did he want?"

"Oh, Edna'd seen Arlette with someone. He wanted to check on it. He's a nice man, and very knowledgeable about paintings. Daddy says he does cartoons for the *Broadshire News.* Did you know?"

Sarah shook her head. She poured boiling water into the tea pot, then removed the baby from her mother's lap and slid her into the high chair. She said carefully, "He didn't ask about Simon, did he?"

"No, why?"

"I just—Sy won't have to be questioned or anything?"

"I should think he already has been."

"Yes, but—you know what I mean."

"As a suspect?" Claire spoke bluntly, and Sarah flashed her an alarmed glance. "I suppose if it turns out she was murdered, everyone who knew her is suspect. But since Simon was in Shillingham, and she died up here—"

"Can he prove he was? In Shillingham?"

"Well, he phoned me, didn't he?"

Sarah said gently, "Look, we *know* Simon. But someone else could say, How do you know he was phoning from Shillingham? He could have been establishing an alibi."

Claire felt chilled. She said with an effort, "If he was expecting to show her the stables, he probably told the station officer she hadn't turned up. Or someone at the railway station could have seen him waiting to meet the train. And when she didn't come, he must have done something else. Hopefully with witnesses." She paused, said, "Oh God!" and took a quick sip of tea.

Sarah laid a hand on hers. "Mum, I'm sorry. I'm making things worse. It was just the way my mind was working. I woke in the night and started panicking about it."

"Motive, means, and opportunity. Isn't that what a murderer needs? Means, we can discount. Anybody can push someone else off a precipice. As to opportunity, he didn't have it. *We* know he was in Shillingham all day, and, please God, plenty of other people do too. Which leaves motive, and what could that be? Simon hasn't a jealous bone in his body and he didn't even know her well. There was no way her death could benefit him financially, and he hasn't any dark secrets she could have discovered. So there, my lud, is the case for the defence."

They held each other's eyes for a moment, then both smiled and the atmosphere eased. Sarah said, "Thanks. I feel a bit better now."

"So do I," Claire admitted. "I'd been worrying about it too, but thinking it through as dispassionately as possible has proved there's nothing to panic about. I hope."

Katy, bored with conversation which didn't include her, and eying the Marmite "soldiers" just out of reach, banged her hand on the tray which lay on the chair and said firmly, "Tea!"

The last of the tension dissolved in laughter.

The flat, having been shut up for thirty-six hours, was stuffy, and Webb flung open all the windows, pausing as he usually did to stare down the hill to the town spread at its foot. The thirty-six hours had been eventful: two missing girls found, one alive, one dead. And two babies born, one of them his godson. He'd accepted that honour with gratitude, but had he thought it through? For that matter, had the Jacksons? Webb, no churchgoer since his youth, realised he'd no idea whether or not the Jacksons attended regularly. Would he have to promise to see Tim had a Christian upbringing? The idea filled him with alarm. Was he *worthy* to be anyone's godfather? It involved more than presents at Christmas and birthdays.

God, he could do without this philosophising! It had been plaguing him ever since he'd learned of the twins' birth. He was alone too much, that was the trouble. Apart from work, he'd little contact with people. His principal hobbies of drawing and painting were solitary ones, involving hours spent in isolation. Alone, yes, but not lonely. Most of the time he was satisfied with his own company; and when he wasn't, until recently he'd had Hannah to turn to. In particular, there came a point in most of his cases, and certainly all the murders, when he needed a disinterested sounding-board to test his theories. Many were the nights he'd lain with Hannah at his side, propounding, discussing, discarding one possibility after another. Arlette Picard might not have been murdered, but her death depressed him, and there were still people he'd interviewed who, for varying reasons, had not told him the truth. And the fact needled him.

If only Hannah were still available, to listen to him, even if not to make love to. He glanced at his watch. Seven o'clock. Would Frobisher be on her doormat again this evening? There was one way to find out. He lifted the phone and dialled her number.

"David, hello. I'm so sorry about the girl. I phoned you last night, but there was no reply."

A more promising opening than he'd expected. "I stayed in Steeple Bayliss. Yes, it's a bad business."

"I sent a note to her parents, but it's hard to know what to say."

"Still harder when you sit across from them, and don't even speak their language."

"You found an interpreter?"

"The university supplied one, but that wasn't what I meant."

"I know." She paused. "You sound depressed."

"I am. It's that stage of the inquiry."

Another pause. Then, "Like to talk it over?"

"Would I!"

"Have you eaten?"

"No, I've only just got back."

"Come down, then. I've plenty for two, if you'll settle for cold meat and salad. Monday fare."

"Couldn't be better. Thanks, Hannah. Give me half an hour."

Her hair was down this time, and she looked altogether more familiar and approachable. His flowers were still in the vase, holding their own. Below the open windows, the gardens of Beechcroft, a legacy from the gracious old house that had once stood on the site, lay bathed in the sunshine which, in the evening of the day, had finally broken through. Surprising how soothing an expanse of green was on tired eyes. And the myriad shades of it, in tree and shrub and grass and plant. It was the colour he found hardest to mix to his satisfaction.

Hannah touched his shoulder, and as he turned put a glass in his hand. "Cheers!"

"Cheers." He smiled at her over the rim of it, his eyes moving over her wide forehead and clear grey eyes, her lightly tanned skin and thick, golden brown hair. She was lovely and he wanted her, but, playing safe, he'd not so much as kissed her cheek. He could take no liberties till she indicated they'd be acceptable—if she ever did. There was a lot of talking to be done before he'd know her exact feelings, and the shadow of Frobisher hovered between them.

As usual, they kept to light topics while they ate. She had laid the table in her minute dining-room, and the formality thus stamped on the meal, compared with trays on their knees, was another warning not to read too much into her offer to talk.

To Webb, salad meant a hunk of lettuce, with perhaps a tomato beside it. This one offered a visual as well as gastronomic delight. In a seasoned wooden bowl nestled bite-sized pieces of raw mushrooms and cauliflower, frond-like beanshoots, glistening radishes, peppers, squares of apple and melon, spindly alfalfa and slender mange-tout, all barely coated with a fragrant dressing in which he detected herbs and garlic. The meat she'd referred to was slices of rare beef. He'd been right there, he reflected, remembering his thoughts in *The Barley Mow.* What he *didn't* know was whether, the day before, Frobisher had shared it with her, and he was certainly not going to ask.

They finished the meal with a piece of Stilton at exactly the right stage of maturity. If this was standard Monday fare he'd call again, but the cheese, like the beef, could be left over from a previous and carefully planned repast.

Hannah carried the coffee to the sitting-room. The room was arranged for summer, with the window rather than the fireplace its focal point, and she put the tray on a table in front of it, closing the window, and lighting a lamp in the far corner of the room. The sun had set, but the sky was still streaked with red and gold, against which the outlines of the trees were etched in silhouette. Webb settled back in his chair with a contented sigh. The coffee was fragrant, the scent of its recent grinding still in the air. They drank it black and unsweetened.

"You want to talk about the case?" Hannah prompted, curling her legs under her in the capacious chair.

He hesitated, his eyes dropping to his coffee cup. Then he

said deliberately, "There are other things I'd rather talk about. Would you mind?"

He could feel her stillness. "Very well," she said.

He had the go-ahead, but didn't know where to start. How *could* he excuse those months of silence following his betrayal? Feeling his way, he said slowly, "It's not enough to say I'm sorry. I've been a fool and a coward. If it's any help, I bitterly regret it."

She didn't speak, merely took another sip of coffee.

"About Susan," he went on with difficulty. "I didn't mean to get involved—it had hurt enough the first time. I suppose I was flattered that she came back. And our relationship was always very physical. Even during the worst times, we still wanted each other. It just—flared up again."

"So if she came back another time?"

At least she was listening. He shook his head vigorously. "Positively not. For a start she wouldn't, but even if she did, it wouldn't happen again. Couldn't. I've learned my lesson, but at too great a cost. Hannah, these last months I've thought about you a great deal, wondered what you were feeling."

"But you didn't bother to find out." No inflection in her voice.

"At first I was too ashamed. And I was sure we'd meet anyway, at the garages or on the stairs. I wanted the first approach to be casual, as easy as possible. I thought if I knocked on your door, you'd shut it in my face."

"A note?"

"Yes, of course I could have written, but what could I say? 'I've been a naughty boy, but I won't do it again?' I'm not good with words, Hannah. Either written or spoken."

"You're not doing too badly."

Was she smiling? There wasn't light enough to see—the lamp was behind her and it was dark beyond the window. He said, "Tell me your side of it."

She bent forward to refill their cups, then sat back, swirling the liquid in her own and looking down at it thoughtfully. "I think I expected it to happen," she said at last. "As soon as you told me she was here. I'd just got back from Europe—remember?"

Yes, he remembered. They'd been in bed at the time.

"But you see, David, I'd no claims on you. That was part of our agreement—we were free to see whomever we chose. I just—hadn't expected it to hurt so much."

He made a movement towards her but she shook her head quickly and he sat back.

"When I saw you together that morning, I was sure you'd phone to explain. I waited all day and all evening, convinced you'd contact me. When you didn't, I assumed firstly that you and Susan were back together, and later, when I heard she'd left Shillingham, that you felt it had been as good a way as any to end our relationship."

"You thought me capable of that?" There was pain in his voice, but she answered levelly, "What else could I think, since you never bothered to explain?"

To which there was no reply. "And Charles Frobisher?" he asked instead. "Where does he fit in?"

There was a long silence. Then she said, "He's asked me to marry him."

Webb flinched and his heart began a slow and heavy pounding. Shock, he told himself. Stupidly, he'd not anticipated that—not seriously. But why not? He put his coffee cup down, forced himself to say lightly, "I thought you weren't the marrying kind?"

"I thought so, too."

"Till Mr. Right came along?" He could hear the bitterness in his voice, and hated himself for it. He added, because he had to, "And are you going to?"

"I don't know."

"Do you love him?" he demanded roughly.

She answered carefully, "I'm very fond of him. He's kind, considerate, good company, interested in the same things as I am. And he loves me."

"So do I." Probably the first time he'd said it. He heard her indrawn breath.

"You have an odd way of showing it."

"Where did you meet him?"

"I've known him for years—he's one of the school governors. But it was at the Christmas concert that we first—came together."

Three months after the fiasco with Susan. *Why* hadn't he approached her before then? Was his damn pride so important that he'd been prepared to lose her? Or had he had the gall to think she'd be waiting whenever he chose to go back? Hannah had her pride, too.

He said accusingly, out of his hurt, "You always said you wouldn't marry."

"Yes. Mainly because I wouldn't give up my career. But with Charles I shouldn't have to."

"He seems wellheeled," he said unforgivably, and was grateful that she didn't reply.

"Tell me, David," she said after a moment, "if we hadn't happened to meet in Steeple Bayliss, would you *ever* have contacted me? Or do you only want me now someone else is interested?"

When he didn't—because he couldn't—answer, she said in a low voice, "I'm sorry, that wasn't fair. I'm as much to blame as you are. Yes"—she raised her voice above his protest—"I am, because I didn't keep to our bargain. The no-strings bit. I believed I was, but I was fooling myself. Not about marriage—I never thought of that. But I expected—and wanted—us to go on as we were, indefinitely. Which was extremely childish."

"Then I was childish, too."

"It was you who ended it. And when you did, I had to rethink everything; my life, my ambitions—my future, I suppose. Because I wasn't as independent as I'd thought."

"Which is why, though you'd not thought of marrying me, you're considering Frobisher."

"I suppose that's it."

He leaned forward urgently. "Hannah, I want you back. I'll do anything you ask, stick to any rules you care to make. Just don't—*please* don't marry Frobisher." He paused. "What did you tell him, when he asked you?"

"That I'd think it over. And I am doing that."

"Have you reached a decision?"

She couldn't tell him that his coming back into her life had blown wide apart any plans she'd contemplated. "Not yet."

"Then can't we start again? Rebuild what we had before?" He took hold of her hand. "Please, Hannah. I know I've been a bastard, but give me another chance."

"I'd have to consider that, too. If you're suggesting we immediately go back to where we were, the answer's no. On the other hand, if you mean literally start again, getting to know each other on a different level, then—perhaps."

He let out his breath on a long sigh, bent his head, and kissed her fingers. "I suppose that's more than I deserve."

"It certainly is! Now," she gently disengaged her hand, "do you want to discuss Arlette, or not? And if so, would a brandy help?"

"I think it would." He smiled, allowing the awkwardness between them to dissipate into less personal topics. She went to the drinks table and he heard the clink of glasses, the liquid being poured. He felt exhausted, mentally and physically, but it was a good feeling, because underlying it was an overwhelming sense of relief. The conversation he'd been dreading for eight months was behind him, and miraculously it seemed he was still in with a chance. Which, as they'd agreed, was far more than he deserved.

CHAPTER 9

"Two items of possible interest, Dave," Chris Ledbetter greeted Webb the next morning. "SOCO report on the going-over of Palfry's car, and a discrepancy in Duncan's statement."

"Sounds promising. What gives?"

"There were some blonde hairs in the car which are highly likely to have come from the dead girl."

"Wow. And he swore he hardly knew her. What about Morgan's?"

"The results aren't through on that one. As to Duncan, we checked his statement and although he *did* have a dental appointment at eleven, it was only a fifteen-minute checkup, which takes us to eleven-fifteen or so. A little early for lunch, wouldn't you say?"

"He probably went home and read the paper for an hour."

"That's what we thought. But as luck would have it, Happy got corroboration from a neighbour, who saw him drive up at a quarter to one. She was sure of the time because she'd just opened the door for her husband, who comes home for lunch every day. 'You can set your clock by him,' she said."

"So that's an hour and a half unaccounted for. And he had his car with him; he could get quite a way in that time."

"Only thing is, Campbell said Arlette was hurrying to meet someone at ten-thirty, which is on the early side."

"Unless she met Duncan afterwards. Where is the dentist, and where's Duncan's house?"

"The surgery's on the main Gloucester road, and the Duncans live just off it."

"Which is the direction Campbell said she was going in. OK, Chris, we'll chase up Duncan and Palfry, and see where that gets us."

Alastair Duncan greeted them with his usual truculence. "I'm sorry the girl's dead," he said brusquely, "but I've already told you all I know."

"As it happens, sir, we know more than you told us," Webb said smoothly.

The man glowered at him. "What, exactly?"

"That although you left the dentist at eleven-twenty, you didn't get home till twelve forty-five."

A wave of heat suffused his face and his eyes flickered. Gotcha! Jackson thought exultantly. He'd always suspected this was the rotten egg.

"I'm sure my wife would tell you—"

"I'm sure she would. But we have an independent witness who saw you return home. So I ask you again, sir, where were you between eleven-twenty and twelve forty-five last Tuesday?"

Duncan hesitated, then lowered his head, clasping his hands tightly on the top of the desk. After a moment he said gruffly, "If I swore to you on oath that it was a purely personal matter and has nothing to do with Arlette Picard, would you accept that?"

"In the circumstances, I'm afraid not."

"What'll happen if I refuse to answer?"

"It's your right, sir. But we may have to ask you to accompany us to the station, to help with our inquiries."

The man's head shot up, his startled eyes meeting Webb's. "Man, I've *told* you—"

"We need proof, sir."

Another pause. Then, "Very well. But I'm not proud of this, and I'm telling you in the strictest confidence. Is that understood?"

"We'll have to use our discretion on that. If as you say it

has nothing to do with the inquiry, there should be no need for it to go further."

"Then I have to tell you that I *did* meet a young lady, but not Miss Picard." The man's face was burning, but he held Webb's eye with angry defiance.

Damn! thought Jackson. Still, so much for that pompous "I'm a married man."

"The lady's name?"

"Must I say?"

"She'll be asked to corroborate, sir."

"Anna Martin. She's—one of my students."

"And where did you meet?"

"She rents a house with three other girls. We—use it sometimes, when the others are out."

"She didn't attend lectures that day?"

"She'd none in the forenoon, so she studied at home, waiting for me."

"Her address?" Webb waited while Jackson wrote it down. "It would have saved time, sir," he said mildly, "if you'd told us this when we first called. We don't appreciate wasting our time."

"I'm sorry," Duncan said grudgingly. "I couldn't see that it had any relevance, and if my wife—"

"Quite. Where is Miss Martin now?"

"On the campus somewhere, in a classroom or the library."

"She's in your department?"

A brief nod.

"And there really is nothing more you can tell us?"

"Nothing, except to repeat this mustn't get out."

"We'll do our best," Webb said enigmatically.

Mrs. Palfry advised them, alarm in her voice, that her husband was manager of a bank in the High Street. "There's nothing wrong, is there?" she added anxiously.

"Just following up our inquiries," Jackson told her, and

replaced the phone, adding to Webb, "It could have been him as easy as Morgan, outside the digs."

"That's immaterial now, Ken. What we need is to pin-point whoever met her last Tuesday, and he—or she—could be any age. Pity there was no diary in that shoulder-bag."

On giving their names at the bank, they were led discreetly to Palfry's office behind its mahogany door. The man rose to greet them, noticeably nervous. In formal rather than casual clothes, he was an imposing figure, used, no doubt, to handing out reassurance or remonstrance as called for to his clients.

"Yes, Chief Inspector? Please, sit down."

Webb and Jackson settled themselves in the comfortable chairs. "It's about your car, sir."

Palfry half-smiled, more an involuntary tic than an expression of amusement. "So I assumed."

"Some long blonde hairs were found in it. And since no one in your family has that colouring, and they very closely match the hair of Arlette Picard—"

"Yes, yes. You don't need to spell it out."

"Something you missed with the brush and dustpan," Webb said impassively. "Amazing, what these chaps come up with."

"I can explain, of course, but it won't be any help to you."

"Suppose you let us decide that, sir."

Palfry had much more assurance here than at home, Webb reflected, but it was a borrowed persona, part of the job. Which was why he preferred to see people in their own homes. It was there you found the true character, augmented by the surroundings he had himself created.

"I didn't lie to you," Palfry went on, "simply bent the truth a little. I see now it was foolish, but to explain in front of my wife and daughters, when I hadn't mentioned the incident—" He spread his hands expressively.

"If you could start at the beginning, sir?"

"Yes. Well, the point was I found the girl attractive, and that worried me. After all, I'm happily married and I love my family. But—well, everything's pretty much routine. The excitement's gone, I'm getting older, and so on." He put a hand to his thinning hair, then leant forward earnestly.

"But I must make it clear I never laid a finger on her. There was no physical contact, nor did I want any. That would've been dangerous, and I'm a cautious man at heart." Another half-smile. "Bank manager mentality, you might say. Arlette brought glamour into my life, but only vicariously—like dreaming of Brigitte Bardot." Even that dated him, Jackson thought.

"Thursdays became special. I'd hurry home and have a quick shave before she arrived. Don't ask me why; I didn't expect her to notice, just wanted to look my best. Pathetic, really."

"And the hairs in the car?" Webb prompted. There was nothing imaginary about them.

"I'm coming to that. About ten days ago I saw her at the bus stop by the university, so I stopped and offered her a lift. It was as harmless as that—I just dropped her off in Farthing Lane on the way home. It's only round the corner from us, as I let slip before."

"And you didn't mention it to your wife?"

"No. Which was stupid, because Arlette might have referred to it later. But it seemed part of my daydream and I didn't want to share it. Added to which, when I got home one of the twins said, 'You're looking very flushed, Dad. Had a heavy date?' It was a joke, naturally, but imagine telling them, after that, that I'd just driven Arlette home. I'd never have heard the end of it." He paused for a moment, remembering.

"So when you asked, in front of them, if she'd been in my car, I panicked. If I'd admitted it, it would have seemed more important than it was."

"And where were you, sir, last Tuesday?"

"Here, as my diary will confirm. I'd a string of appointments all day. The only time I left my desk was for a quick lunch with some friends whom I meet every week. I can give you their names."

So last Tuesday, which was now all that mattered, Rob Palfry had been at his desk. Webb and Jackson emerged from the bank with yet another name eliminated from their rapidly dwindling list of suspects.

"Chief Inspector! Good morning!" Tom Marshbanks had stopped in front of them. "Or good afternoon, I should say, but I consider it morning till I've had my lunch. I'm on my way for it now. Would you and the sergeant care to join me?"

"Well, sir—" Webb hesitated, but he saw the light in Ken's eye, and he liked Tom Marshbanks. "That's very kind of you."

"Excellent. I usually go to a wine bar just along the road. They pride themselves on traditional English cooking, and do an excellent game pie."

Webb grinned. "A bit more up-market than we're used to, but it sounds tempting."

The Pickwick had an appropriately Victorian atmosphere, with sawdust on the floor and a succession of small rooms leading out of each other. Ancient farm implements hung round the walls, emphasising Steeple Bayliss' long history as an agricultural centre, and in the middle of the innermost room stood an enormous chimney, its huge grate filled with intricately wrought fire irons.

The game pies were served individually in earthenware dishes, accompanied by baked potatoes and salad. The three men ate with relish, Webb and Jackson opting for beer rather than the house wine Tom Marshbanks ordered.

"How's the inquiry going?" he asked, as the cheese board was produced. "We were distressed to learn of the girl's death."

"We're not making much progress at the moment," Webb admitted. Since his host was young Simon's father, he felt able to speak frankly.

Marshbanks helped himself to a biscuit. "Simon's in the clear, I take it? Officially, I mean."

For all the lightness of the question, Webb sensed the anxiety behind it.

"No question of that. We had to check," he added apologetically, "but luckily when Arlette didn't arrive, he went along to the tennis club and, I imagine, worked off his pique there. Any number of people are ready to vouch for him."

"Thank God," said Simon's father.

"How did your dinner-party with the Warwicks go?" Webb asked, only to change the subject, though the figure of the professor lingered in his mind.

"Not too well, actually. Bernard seemed under a strain."

"That was the impression we got. Any idea why?"

Marshbanks was a truthful man, but he found himself hedging. "Not really. I think his wife's worried, though." He paused. "What's your interest in him, Webb?"

Webb shrugged. "He's in the clear for Tuesday, so it's not that. I just have this gut feeling the man's a walking time-bomb. Don't ask me why."

Minutes later the two detectives took their leave, embarrassed by Marshbanks' insistence on paying for their meal. "Not trying to bribe you!" he assured them, with a grin strongly reminiscent of his son's. "Just happy to stand lunch for Simon's colleagues. Good hunting!"

He watched them thoughtfully as they threaded their way between the tables, Webb tall and lanky, Jackson much slighter. And he thought uneasily of what Claire had told him about Bernard and the Frenchwoman. Like her, he'd been inclined to discount it, but even if Daphne were right, he could see no obligation to repeat the story to the police. Bernard was in the clear over Arlette's death, which was surely all that concerned them. But the phrase Webb had used—a walking time-bomb—struck Marshbanks as strangely apposite, though he didn't know why, either.

With an impatient shake of his head, he dismissed the idea and signalled to the waitress for the bill.

On the way back to the car later that afternoon, Webb stopped impulsively at a florist's, went inside, and emerged, looking faintly embarrassed, with an azalea plant covered in pink buds. This he thrust into Jackson's hands.

"For Millie," he said.

"That's very good of you, guv. Thank you. But how about giving it to her yourself? I'm popping in to see her when we get back—why not come along? You might get a glimpse of the babies, if you're lucky."

"Oh, you don't want me butting in," Webb began hastily, but mention of the babies gave weight to Jackson's repeated invitation. It was time he made his godson's acquaintance. "Well, if you're quite sure," he capitulated.

So it was that, an hour and a half later, he found himself where he'd never expected to be, in the maternity wing of Shillingham General. And he tried to forget that this was where, eight months previously, Susan had spent her working day.

Millie's bed was half way down the ward. She was sitting in a chair beside it, her face wreathed in smiles. "Mr. Webb! What a pleasant surprise!"

"The governor bought you a plant," Jackson explained as Webb awkwardly handed it over, "so I said he should come along, too. How are you, love?"

Millie was exclaiming with delight over the azalea. "And it will last so much longer than cut flowers. It's ever so good of you."

"Matter of fact," said Jackson wickedly, "I think it's young Timothy he's really come to see!"

"Oh, he's lovely, Mr. Webb—they both are. I'm so glad you'll be his godfather. Timothy David, we're calling him. Ken, love, take him along to the nursery and show him where they are."

The nursery had a glass wall behind which visitors were confined. Ken told one of the nurses which babies they'd come to see, and two cots were wheeled over to the glass. Very little of the twins was visible. In each cot a small, tightly cocooned figure lay on its side. Each had orangey red fluff on top of its head, and tightly closed eyes.

"Tim's on the right," Jackson volunteered.

"They're—great," Webb said, inadequately, he felt. He'd never seen such young children before, and the minuteness of them took him by surprise. Subconsciously he'd been expecting the plump, rounded limbs of babies several months old. As he looked down at his tiny godson, the infant opened his eyes, turned his head, and stared straight up at the glass screen.

"There!" Jackson exclaimed delightedly, "He's looking at you!"

Webb had no idea how far the baby's vision went, nor if light reflected on the glass made his own face invisible. But for several awe-filled moments it seemed that the child was holding his gaze. Then the little face twisted in a spasm of wind, the minute lips made sucking motions, and the eyes closed again.

"He's great, Ken," Webb repeated, this time with more conviction. "You must be very proud of them."

CHAPTER 10

Beryl said, "Are you sure you feel up to this seminar, dear?"

Her voice reached Bernard as the buzzing of an insect, irritating, but meaningless. His thoughts, as always, were centred on Cécile. He'd phoned the hotel, but it was Gaston who answered. Confining himself to formal condolences, Bernard was shaken by his surge of hatred towards this man who was keeping his love from him. He considered asking to speak to her, but natural caution prevailed. Yet, poor sweet, she must be longing for him as he was for her, specially during this waiting period, while the police looked into Arlette's death.

"Bernard?" Beryl spoke more loudly, and he frowned, turning his head towards her. "I said are you well enough to come to Melbray?"

"*Well* enough?" he repeated irritably. "Of course I'm well enough—there's nothing wrong with me." Why couldn't she go away—permanently? Yet in fairness, she wasn't the problem Gaston posed. Once he explained, she'd leave all right. She'd too much pride to hang on where she wasn't wanted. Fleetingly, he was aware of pity. Still, he'd given her ten years.

"Have you got your notes ready?"

He smiled with genuine amusement. "I don't need notes on Brouge. I know it by heart."

Beryl didn't like the look of him at all. There was a feverish heat about him, apparent in his flushed cheeks and glittering eyes, and she knew he heard little that she said to him. Today, midway through the week-long course on French literature, was assigned to Bernard as world authority on

Brouge. *Had* he planned what to say? Beryl had the gnawing fear that he would stand in front of his audience, staring blankly into space. And then what would she do?

She felt desperately, most horribly alone, a sensation which, though familiar before her marriage, had over the last ten years been blessedly rare. Unwillingly she thought back to those daunting times when she had to make decisions and deal with things completely on her own; the panic on entering a room, or speaking to a truculent tradesman, even querying change in the supermarket. Though Bernard hadn't been constantly beside her—in fact, looking back, very seldom—his ring on her finger and his presence in the background had given her confidence. Now, it was rapidly evaporating. And she *couldn't* say any more to Claire. What would she think? She owed it to Bernard to keep going, to pretend nothing was wrong if he didn't want to discuss it, and try to still any incipient gossip before it could take hold.

"If you're ready, then," she said brightly, "it's time we were going. Claire will be waiting."

Claire, getting into the back of the car, also gave Bernard a wary glance. He hadn't returned her greeting, though Beryl covered the omission with her chatter. She'd half-expected him to withdraw from the course and had a replacement in mind, should it become necessary. Watching his face in the driving mirror, Claire was filled with unease. His eyes were glazed and the tremor in his hands made her doubt his fitness to drive, let alone to lecture. She guessed he was doing the one, as perhaps he'd do the other, automatically.

"Has Simon been in touch?" Beryl prattled. "Any more news of developments?"

"No, nothing." Claire, watching Bernard, saw the spasm go through him. What *was* the connection between himself and the Picards? And had it extended to their daughter?

Bernard thought: Brouge. It was Cécile who discovered him, not I. He remembered the mild spring evening all those years ago, when they'd joined the throngs of Parisians strolling by the river and paused at the stalls of the *bouquinistes.*

"Look what I've found!" she'd exclaimed. He could see her now in his mind's eye, not the Cécile of today, with her silver wings of hair, but the slim, bubbly girl who had so entranced him. "Marcel Brouge," she'd said. "A first edition. Have you heard of him?"

He hadn't, and, taking the book from her, flicked through it, becoming instantly engrossed. Later, having read it, he'd made inquiries about the author, and found little was known of him. But it was only now, as he guided the car through green English lanes, that he realised at least part of his obsession with Brouge stemmed from the connection with Cécile. The long-dead Frenchman had been Bernard's last, tenuous link with his lost love. It was fitting, therefore, that now, when he'd found her again, he should be giving this lecture. Full circle, as it were. If she weren't so distressed about Arlette, he'd have suggested she come to hear it.

His musings had, as Claire suspected, brought them without conscious thought to the manor house. At the gates, a noticeboard advertised the current programme. Under today's date, he read: "Marcel Brouge, His Life and Works. Professor Bernard Warwick, MA St. And, Ph.D. R'dg, DU Paris."

He guided the car along the drive to the space reserved for the visiting lecturer. Inside, someone waited to greet him, and, free at last of his wife and Claire, he left them without a glance.

In silence, Beryl and Claire went to their office. Daphne looked up as they entered, her eyes going from one solemn face to the other. Had Claire passed on her disquieting news? She flashed her a look of anxious inquiry, and Claire, interpreting it, shook her head.

"I hope the Prof's on form," Daphne gushed in relief. "There's quite a crowd in there—more than came to Proust."

Beryl lowered herself slowly into her chair, and Daphne eyed her uncertainly. Despite Claire's assurance, she looked as if she knew of her husband's lapse. Silence had again fallen, and again Daphne strove to break it.

"I say, Claire, would it be poss to swap duties on Friday? I've a date with the fang-merchant—six fillings, forsooth—but I could manage P.M."

Claire said with an effort, "If I were you, I'd take the day off. Don't worry, I can cover for you. I've nothing on till the evening."

"Gosh, are you sure? You are a brick—thanks most awfully." Daphne flashed her a toothy smile, gathered up the papers she'd been assembling, and hurried out of the room.

"God give me strength!" Beryl exploded. "The way that woman fawns over you, you'd think she had lesbian tendencies."

Claire stared at her, her smile fading. She was as shocked by the fact that it was Beryl voicing the sentiment as by the sentiment itself. "*Daphne?* I doubt if she even knows what they are."

"In her parlance, then," Beryl said savagely, "she has a *pash* on you. A crush. It boils down to the same thing."

"It most certainly does not!" Claire said hotly. "And anyway, that's nonsense. You know as well as I do that Daphne's the most innocent, gullible—"

"God, I'm sorry, Claire." Beryl put her hands to her face. "I didn't mean it. I don't know what's the matter with me."

Claire looked at her for a moment, letting her indignation subside. "You're worried out of your mind, that's what's the matter with you."

"Yes," Beryl said flatly. Why deny it?

"You still think Bernard doesn't love you?" Did she owe it to Beryl to repeat Daphne's tale? But not now; Daphne was in enough disfavour.

"It's not so much that; I'm sure he's on the verge of a breakdown. There's a contained excitement about him, as though he's waiting for something to happen."

"And he won't see a doctor?"

"No, he gets furious when I suggest it."

Claire glanced at her watch. "Tell you what. If you can hold the fort for a while—and be nice to Daphne!—I'll slip into the lecture room and see how it's going." Quite often, if they weren't too busy, one or other of them would sit in on a seminar. Claire enjoyed the stimulation, and Beryl incorporated it into her self-improvement scheme.

"If he's managing all right," she added, "you can probably stop worrying." She wished she could believe that.

"Bless you, Claire," Beryl said gratefully. "That would be a help. And please forget what I said about Daphne. I'm fond of her, too."

Claire's heart was beating uncomfortably as she paused outside the lecture room. Then, holding her breath, she pushed open the door, slipped inside, and took a seat in the back row. If Bernard saw her, he gave no sign. He was still in the introductory stage of the lecture, a general résumé which would be enlarged on throughout the day.

"At the age of twenty-two," he was saying, "Brouge fell violently in love with Jeanne Collière, an apothecary's daughter, but she jilted him. Although there were many other women in his life, he never felt for them as he had for Jeanne, nor did he ever marry." He went on talking, but Claire was only half-listening, concentrating on his form of speech rather than the words, on his mannerisms and movements on the platform. Though a lectern had been provided, he'd pushed it aside, and the desk in front of him was bare of papers. He was, however, repeatedly sipping from the water in his glass. She must send someone to top up the carafe.

"It was about this time that he wrote his bestknown novel, *Le Serpent*, and later in life, when his mental illness developed, people referred back to that early work as the first instance in which his phobia about snakes manifested itself."

He was speaking like a wellrehearsed actor, Claire thought; one who had played the part throughout a long run and knew his lines so thoroughly that he didn't have to think about them.

To some extent she was wrong. Bernard indeed knew his

talk by heart, but today as he delivered it, it struck him with an import so startling, yet at the same time so obvious, he was amazed he'd not seen it before. *He and Brouge shared parallel lives.* They'd both loved deeply, and suffered as a consequence. Both were brilliant—no false modesty on that score—and each had balanced precariously on the edge of sanity. But there the comparison ended. For Brouge had toppled over, and, convinced his body was filled with snakes, ended his days in an asylum for the insane. While in Bernard's own case, Cécile's return had saved him.

As he continued with his delivery, Bernard considered the delusion. There was something about snakes, something primeval, atavistic. Man's most ancient enemy, the cause of his downfall. And the primitive stem of the human cerebrum, so he had read, was called the reptilian brain. That pleased him, for it vindicated Brouge, who had indeed had something of the serpent inside him.

He recalled his own fantasy of his mind crumbling, hidden behind his smoothly impassive face. Perhaps it was his *reptile* brain that threatened the rest, seeking to destroy from within?

Claire's eyes moved from Bernard's commanding figure to his audience. Seated where she was, she could at best see their profiles, but each one seemed engrossed. Occasionally there was the scratching of a pen or a turning page, as some particular comment or example was noted down. She accepted that, had she not had previous doubts about Bernard's condition, nothing in his bearing or delivery would have given rise to them. There was a measure of comfort in that, to pass on to Beryl.

Hannah settled back in her deck chair and prepared for a pleasantly idle afternoon. In front of her, separated by high netting, the girls of the Ashbourne tennis team were knocking up with their opponents from St. Anne's. The soft, rhythmic plopping of the balls, the occasional call of "Yours!" formed, with the droning of a plane far overhead, the quintessential sounds of summer. Forming the thought, Hannah smiled to herself. They could keep their leather on willow; to her mind, cricket was boring and tennis the perfect spectator sport.

But she was not only indulging herself. The match against St. Anne's was a major fixture in the term, and the presence of someone other than the games staff was much appreciated by the players. Added to which, Hannah reckoned she'd earned her treat. The last two weeks had been a strain, exacerbated by an outbreak of measles; while the re-entry of David into her life had also brought attendant problems.

She reached into her bag for sunglasses, recalling their talk on Monday evening. His spontaneous statement that he loved her had, she suspected, surprised himself as much as her. He'd never committed himself before, and it was Charles' proposal that had goaded him into it.

"Good afternoon, Miss James," said a voice above her, and she gave an exclamation. Charles had materialised out of her musings to stand beside her chair.

"Hello! What brings you here?"

"I dropped in those papers for the report. Your secretary told me where to find you."

A prefect, having seen his approach, arrived with another deck chair, which she set up next to Hannah's. Charles smiled at her with his usual charm. "Thank you, my dear. I mustn't stay long, but I'll watch the first couple of games."

The umpire had taken her position, the knocking up ended, and the players tossed for service. Charles said quietly, "You know why I'm really here, don't you?"

Of course she knew. The ten days he had given her to reach a decision were up. They should have been enough. If she hadn't met David again, would she have accepted him? The possibility filled her with panic, a reaction leaving her answer in no doubt. Yet she regretted being pressed to give it. She enjoyed Charles' company; he was sophisticated and amusing, an attentive escort. Furthermore, he shared far more of her interests than David did. David was a home-loving man, busy in his work and liking to relax in the evenings. In the last few months, Charles had taken her about more than David had in three years—to concerts, theatres, dinner-dances. She'd met his friends, and knew, from their attitude towards her, that they expected Charles to marry her and approved his choice.

On the court, Angie Markham sent a backhand skimming over the net to land millimetres inside the back line. As her opponent reached for it, missed, and skidded into the netting, Hannah joined in the burst of applause. All round the court, scattered groups of spectators sat on the grass. There was no one within earshot of herself and Charles, and to all appearances the deputy Head and the Chairman of the Board of Governors were simply watching the tennis. What was more natural?

"Hannah?" he prompted. "Have you made up your mind?"

She sighed and turned to him. "I wish I didn't have to," she said with a wry smile.

If only, she thought guiltily, she could enjoy a relaxed, uncommitted companionship with them both. The two men were opposites, but they appealed to different sides of her personality.

Charles said, "It wouldn't be such a radical change. You'd still have the school, and we'd go out and about just as we have been doing."

But as his wife, living in his home, she would no longer be her own mistress, free, during the long summer holidays, to fly as the mood took her to Greece, the Canaries, Paris; to eat what and when she liked, watch films on television till the small hours, or retire to bed early with a book. And, the most fundamental change of all, David Webb would be out of her life. Permanently.

When she didn't speak, he went on: "Let me plead my case again. You've been totally honest, and I appreciate it. You say though you're fond of me, you don't love me. Fair enough, I can accept that. Because although I do love you, it's not what

I felt for Mary. I'm being honest, too." His wife had died ten years ago. "Nevertheless, Hannah, we're *good* together. Why not enjoy what we have?"

On the court, a world removed from her by more than the netting, Ashbourne had taken the first set. Hannah realised guiltily she'd registered none of it. Briefly, unwillingly, she tried to picture herself as Charles' wife. And failed.

"It has to be no, Charles," she said softly. "I'm very sorry. I've had my freedom too long now to contemplate giving it up. But I've enjoyed your company and our time together very much. I hope we can still be friends."

He was leaning forward in his chair, hands clasped between his knees, seemingly intent on the tennis. His eyes, too, were hidden behind sunglasses. "You're quite sure?"

"I'm afraid so. I'm sorry."

"I shall try again," he said. "Not immediately; we both need to take a step back and survey the situation. But as long as you're not anyone else's wife, I shall go on hoping one day you'll be mine."

Hannah felt her eyes smart, and for the first time wished they were alone, so that she could reach for his hand. "Don't mind too much," she said.

He smiled slightly. "I'd better go. I've an appointment at three. See you at the next meeting, no doubt. Goodbye, Hannah."

"Goodbye." She watched him as he walked towards the main gates, a tall, straight figure, immaculate in navy blazer and pale blue trousers. A tumult of feelings inside her fought for supremacy—regret, pity, but, coming out uppermost, a sense of relief. However painful it had been, she knew she had made the right decision. She was her own woman again.

With a sigh, she settled back and at last gave her full attention to the tennis.

At Melbray, Bernard's seminar was drawing to a close, with several among his audience determined to devote more study to the neglected Brouge. Beryl and Claire, their own work finished, slipped into the back of the room to wait for him. Beryl was anxious to satisfy herself that Claire's morning assessment held good. Watching him intently, she was not too sure. He spoke fluently, sometimes amusingly, but his eyes had the glazed look she had come to dread, which meant that his thoughts were elsewhere. At least there was no sign of disquiet among his audience. To all appearances, they seemed enthralled by what he was saying. Let it be all right, she prayed instinctively. Let nothing go wrong at this stage.

Bernard finished to prolonged and enthusiastic applause which seemed to take him by surprise. He half-smiled, inclined his head, and turned to leave the stage. But his audience had questions.

"One moment, Professor. About Jeanne Collière: did he have any contact with her in later life? I mean, is her influence apparent in his later work?"

Bernard hesitated, and Beryl held her breath. After a seemingly endless pause, he said, "I'm sorry, could you repeat the question?"

The man did so and Claire watched, appalled, as Bernard patently tried to channel his thoughts in a specific direction. The question was simple enough, and she didn't doubt he knew the answer. The problem was that he wasn't prepared for it. Confident with his wellknown text, any deviation requiring original thought, however basic, seemed to confuse him. Stumblingly he began to reply, gaining more confidence as he went along. But both women had registered the ripple of surprise that ran through the room.

As if to test him, someone else raised a point, and again Bernard struggled to express himself. After his previous fluency, his difficulty was embarrassing. Beryl breathed a sigh of relief as someone walked on the platform to propose a vote of thanks—*why* couldn't he have got up sooner?—and Bernard, still looking bemused, was shepherded away.

"What's with this guy?" demanded an American voice in the row in front. "All day he's clued up, now suddenly he dries. What gives?"

Claire, with a glance at Beryl's stricken face, rose to her feet and, taking her friend's arm, led her out of the room. She wished passionately that they'd come in her car; the thought of entrusting themselves to Bernard's driving filled her with alarm, and she wondered if there were some way of avoiding it. In the event, Beryl forestalled her.

Bernard was standing in the hall waiting for them, and they saw the puzzlement of the man beside him. He turned with relief as they came up.

"Ah, there you are, ladies. A fascinating day, as I was telling Professor Warwick. I'm sure he inspired many of his listeners to read Brouge. We're most grateful to him for coming along."

Beryl took Bernard's arm. "You look tired, dear," she said firmly. "I'll drive home."

To Claire's surprise, he made no demur, and they walked out into the warm afternoon. Moving like a sleepwalker, he allowed Beryl to guide him to the car and help him inside.

"I only heard snatches," Claire said, gamely backing Beryl's semblance of normality, "but it was fascinating, Bernard. I found myself wondering, since so little was known of Brouge, how you first came across him?"

He'd been fastening his seat-belt, but his head reared up. Another question, she thought in alarm; she shouldn't have asked. But apparently this answer lay near the surface.

"When I was studying in Paris," he said, a quiver in his voice, "someone saw a book of his on a stall and handed it to me."

"And that was it?" Claire was genuinely interested. "It all stemmed from that?"

There was a pause while Beryl started the car. Then Bernard repeated dreamily, "It all stemmed from that."

Claire dared ask no more.

It had been an uncomfortable day, and Beryl was glad it was over. Bernard, exhausted, had retired to bed immediately after supper. When she herself went up, he was deeply asleep, but there was a copy of *Le Serpent* on the bedside table. She'd have thought he'd had enough of Brouge today.

She had a bath, hoping that the warm water would soothe away the edginess which made her skin prickle and her nerves twitch. She'd told Claire, Bernard seemed to be waiting for something; now, he'd infected her with a sense of fearful anticipation, though of what she had no idea.

It had been so sudden, this decline of his. She thought back, trying to remember when first she'd noticed it. Of course—it was the day they went next door for dinner. When was that? A week last Saturday? Until then, there'd been no sign of anything wrong. She recalled Claire suggesting that the French girl's disappearance might have worried him, but he'd shown no distress when he first told her of it.

She went softly into the bedroom, brushed her hair, and climbed in her own bed. Though she switched off the lamp, there was a full moon and its silvery light seeped through the curtains like ghostly daylight. Beryl lay down, her mind revolving round the day's happenings like a hamster on a wheel.

She'd shocked Claire with her comment about Daphne. She hadn't meant it, either, but there was something about the woman that, especially today, had irritated her. Several times she'd looked up to find those round brown eyes staring at her with an expression Beryl couldn't define but which nevertheless made her uneasy.

And then those awful, tense minutes when Bernard had floundered, seemingly unable to comprehend a simple question. The possibility of mental illness must be faced, but what could she do about it? And *could* it come on as suddenly and devastatingly as this? It wasn't as though he'd had a shock of any kind.

In the next bed Bernard stirred suddenly. "The reason I killed my wife," he said, loudly and distinctly, "was because she loved me."

CHAPTER 11

"Dick here, guv. Sorry to be so long coming back on Morgan's car, but I reckon it was worth it. I think we've got him."

Webb leant over Chris Ledbetter's desk. "What did you find?"

"Irrefutable evidence of the girl's presence."

"But he admitted that. He—"

"Hold on a minute. There were fibres from the linen skirt, and she wore that for the first time the day she vanished."

Webb let out his breath on a long sigh. "Cheers, Dick. I'll be in touch."

He put the phone down, meeting Ledbetter's eye. "Something positive at last. Hang on a sec, Chris, while I double-check. Got the landlady's phone number?"

Minutes later Webb had confirmed that Arlette did not put on her new clothes as soon as she bought them; they were worn for the first time when she went out to her death.

"As I thought. Mr. Morgan has some explaining to do, and this time he can do it here. Could Happy go and pick him up? Only for questioning, mind."

"Great. It's about time I got in on the act!"

When Webb and Ledbetter reached the interview room, Morgan was sitting at the table staring at its pitted surface. A uniformed constable stood impassively inside the door. As it opened, Morgan stumbled to his feet and started to bluster, but his heart evidently wasn't in it. His pasty skin gleamed with sweat.

Webb cut across his protests. "Sit down, Mr. Morgan. This is Inspector Ledbetter. He has some questions for you."

Morgan subsided, scowling. He watched in silence as Ledbetter propped his crutches against the wall and swung to one of the chairs. Fellow looked like a film star, he thought disgustedly, but he wasn't underestimating Webb.

"Now, Mr. Morgan," the glamour boy began, "we have reason to believe you've not been completely honest with us."

"We've been all over that. I admitted I took her to—"

Ledbetter raised his voice. "When was the last time you saw Miss Picard?"

Morgan moistened his lips. "The night before she went missing. We had a Chinese meal, then I took her home."

"What was she wearing, Mr. Morgan?"

"*Wearing?* How the hell should I know? I never notice what women wear—ask my wife!"

"What she was *not* wearing was the linen skirt and blue top she'd just bought. Mrs. King was very clear on that."

"So?"

"She wore those for the first time the next day."

"All right, I'm not arguing with you."

Chris Ledbetter leant forward, his hands clasped on the table. "But you see, Mr. Morgan, fibres from the skirt were found in your car. You understand what that means, don't you?" Morgan stared at him, his small eyes as expressionless as pebbles. "It means," Ledbetter continued softly, "that she must have been in your car on the *Tuesday*, the day she disappeared."

Morgan said tonelessly, "Oh God," and ran a finger round the inside of his collar.

"So perhaps you'll tell us the truth this time. Third time lucky, shall we say?" The sarcasm in the detective's voice brought no reaction. Morgan scarcely seemed to hear him.

"Oh God!" he said again, on a rising note, and then, "I didn't kill her, I swear it!"

"The truth," Ledbetter repeated implacably.

Morgan took a handkerchief from his pocket and wiped his forehead. At the small table in the corner, Happy Hopkins, too, paused, his pen in his hand. Now, thought Webb, perhaps we'll get the answer.

"All right, I did meet her. We fixed it the night before."

"Go on."

Morgan said desperately, "Can I smoke?"

Ledbetter raised his eyebrows at Webb, a noted nonsmoker. He nodded. "If it'll help."

Morgan reached in his pocket, producing a silver cigarette case and lighter. Not the usual class of villain, Happy thought, watching from his corner. Crumpled packets and a box of matches were the norm. Morgan lit up, inhaled deeply, and seemed to take confidence from it. He offered the case to the officers, but they declined.

"I wanted her," he said then. "I always had. You probably guessed that. And she must have *known*. Girls do, don't they? I thought she was teasing, playing the innocent, but looking back, I'm not so sure." He tapped his cigarette on the metal ashtray. "When we started going for a meal, I assumed one thing would lead to another, but I was wrong. She seemed almost shocked when I kissed her. It took me aback, I can tell you—damn it, I thought she'd be expecting it. Perhaps she thought I was wining and dining her out of the goodness of my heart. Anyway, all I got was a brief peck and no more. She was far more interested in teaching me French grammar." He grimaced ruefully. "And she insisted on calling me 'monsieur.' As time went on she relaxed a bit, though I still had to toe the line. And of course, the more she played hard to get, the more I wanted her."

"Go on," Ledbetter prompted into the growing silence.

Morgan stubbed out his cigarette and lit another. "The main trouble was never having a long enough time together. I daren't be too late arriving at bowls, and in any case the car was limiting. I thought if I could have her to myself for a while, where we wouldn't be hurried or disturbed, things would work out. After all, most girls would be flattered to be with a man in my position."

The policemen avoided each other's eyes as Morgan, unaware that he'd said anything questionable, drew deeply on his cigarette.

"I waited till I'd a legitimate reason to be out of the office. Then, that Monday night, I suggested a run into the country the next day. She agreed, provided she was back by lunchtime. We arranged to meet in The Lamb and Flag carpark at ten-thirty."

He stared at his cigarette, remembering. "I was there first. I can see her now, coming towards me with her hair bouncing on her shoulders and that spring in her step girls have when they know they're being watched. As she slipped in beside me, she leaned across and gave me a quick kiss—the first time she'd taken the initiative. Then she smiled and said, 'You like my new clothes?' " He ran a hand across his eyes. The policemen waited in silence.

"She sat in the car while I did the inspections. I went through them in record time, I can tell you. I was at the stage when I could hardly keep my hands off her. There was a kind of bloom about her, somehow. And the kiss, coupled with the fact that she'd agreed to come—well, I was sure she knew what I had in mind."

"And you were wrong again?"

"Couldn't have been more so. I drove along the Gloucester road and turned off over the heath. After a while we got out and I spread a rug on the grass. And that was where things started going wrong. She flatly refused to play, insisting she'd thought we were going for a drive. The hell of it is, she might genuinely have misunderstood. It's hard to tell, with foreigners. There are innuendos, colloquialisms which would be explicit to an English girl but could have been lost on Arlette. At the time, though, I didn't think of that. I thought she'd deliberately led me on, and I was mad as hell."

But he hadn't raped her, Webb thought. According to the

PM she was *virgo intacta*, which had come as a surprise. "So what happened?" he asked quietly.

"I did my damnedest to persuade her. Hell, I was pretty worked up by then, and there she was, fighting me off and insisting she'd a train to catch. Not at all what I'd planned. I lost my temper, started shouting at her, and she burst into tears. In the end I scooped up the rug, threw it in the back of the car, and drove off without her. I remember shouting something about finding her own way back, and serve her right."

"Or did she run away, and you went after her?"

"No, as God's my witness it was the way I told you. Indirectly, I did cause her death. I accept that. I shouldn't have left her there; it was a lousy thing to do, but it never entered my head to *harm* her. Ever since I heard what happened, I've been going through hell."

"And what do you think *did* happen, Mr. Morgan?"

"She was making her way down to the road, wasn't she, to hitch a lift back to town. But the slope's pretty steep there, and those high heels would have been lethal." He paused and added, "Literally lethal. One must have broken under her and pitched her forward."

It was a pretty astute deduction. Too astute. The broken heel had not been mentioned in press reports. Webb said softly, "You found her, didn't you?"

Morgan spread his hands resignedly. "I thought you'd get round to that. When I heard she was missing, I drove back to look for her. Damn it, wouldn't you? No one saw me—they weren't searching so far afield."

"When was this, Mr. Morgan?" Webb interrupted.

"The Thursday evening, as soon as I heard. I parked where I had before and started walking and calling for her. I realised she mightn't answer if she knew it was me, but I had to try. The Nailsworth road wasn't far away, and I guessed she'd have made for it. And eventually I found her." He stared down at the table. "All right, I should have told you.

But it wouldn't have helped Arlette. She was dead. I imagine her neck broke when she fell."

Webb studied his downcast face. "What was your reaction when you found her?"

"Horror, guilt, then panic. If I reported finding her, you'd wonder how I knew where to look. And though she died because I left her, it hadn't been intentional."

"An anonymous call would have been better than nothing."

"They can be traced, can't they? I daren't risk it. Anyway, you were bound to find her some time."

"So you were content to let her parents go on worrying and hoping—"

"No!" The word was a shout and Morgan put his head in his hands. "Not content," he added more quietly. "But I had my wife to consider, and—"

"You should have thought of that before," Ledbetter said primly, and Morgan flashed him a look of dislike. "Did you touch the body at all?"

"There was no point. I climbed down, praying she'd still be alive, but when it was clear she wasn't, I just left her." He paused. "There was one thing I did. Her little scarf had come off and was lying half under her. I pulled it out, using my handkerchief, and stuck it on a bush beside her. I thought someone might see it from the road."

"Hardly, at sixty miles an hour."

Morgan shrugged. "Anyway, gentlemen, that really is the lot. I behaved badly, I don't deny it, and as a result a girl died. I'll have to live with that for the rest of my life."

Nigel Morgan had waited for his statement to be typed, signed it, and thankfully left.

"So that's it." Chris Ledbetter leant back in his chair with a contented sigh. "Case closed. Well done, Dave. I'm grateful for your help."

Webb sighed also, but not with satisfaction. "The devil of it is, I don't think it's over."

Ledbetter straightened. "You're not saying you don't believe him?"

"Oh, I think it was accidental death, and that'll be the verdict."

"So what's worrying you?"

"I wish I knew. Call it a hunch. I've a feeling that the girl's death was only the starting point, though of what, I'm damned if I know."

Ledbetter smiled crookedly. "You should try swinging a pendulum!"

"Sounds barmy, I agree. But there are ripples spreading from it that haven't been explained. I just don't think we've seen the end of it."

"So what do you propose to do?"

"God knows. Go back to Shillingham and put my head in the sand." He paused. "But I'll breathe more easily when the body's released and they all go back to France."

"What could possibly go wrong now?"

"If I knew that, Chris, I shouldn't feel so helpless. You must have had cases that leave you dissatisfied; that's probably all it is."

"Well, whatever you say, I'm grateful for your help. I'll do the same for you some day. Now, let's go and have a drink. That'll cheer you up."

And Webb, pushing his reservations aside, nodded in agreement.

Usually, the days Bernard came home for lunch were the highlight of her week. Today, Beryl was dreading it. All night and all morning, his words had rung in her head. *The reason I killed my wife—the reason I killed my wife—*

Of course he'd been talking in his sleep, and of course he'd not known what he was saying. But the fact that he'd said it meant it must be in his mind. Sometimes, when she reached this point, she was able to dismiss the whole episode as nonsense. If everyone took seriously what was said or done in dreams . . . But at others, her response was less logical; because over the last week Bernard's manner had become more and more unbalanced, and to her horror she realised she was afraid of him.

He came into the house and without a word seated himself at the table. Beryl said, "Plaice and parsley sauce today." It struck her as the most banal of remarks at this crisis point, but he answered automatically, "Very nice, dear." It was an echo of his old self, the self which had disappointed her by its lack of appreciation, but whose return, now, would have filled her with joy. And because of that normal phrase in the face of such gross abnormality, she said impulsively, "Tell me what's wrong, Bernard. Please."

He raised his head and his eyes found her face. As she watched, their blankness shifted into focus and he said tiredly, "I'm sorry, Beryl. Very, very sorry."

"But what *is* it?" She sat down beside him, putting a hand on his. Though she felt it tremble, he didn't move away. She went on gently, "I only want what's best for you, but lately my just being here seems to upset you."

"Because you love me," he said. She gasped, recoiling as though he had struck her from the phrase that haunted her, and he left it unexplained, seeming to think it explained itself. Yet frightened as she was, she must pursue it; this might be her last chance.

"I'm your wife. Is it wrong to love you?"

He sighed, pushing his plate away untouched. "You're right," he said, "I owe you, at very least, an explanation. I've tried to be good to you, Beryl, and I hope you've been happy. It's no fault of yours that I couldn't love you; I'd no love to give. It's belonged to someone else for thirty years."

"I didn't know that," she whispered.

"There was no point in telling you. I never dreamed I'd see her again."

Comprehension came slowly. "And now you have?"

"Yes. Don't judge me too harshly. It's beyond my control."

"Who—" Beryl's voice croaked. She cleared her throat and said more strongly, "Who is she?"

"Cécile Picard."

"*Picard?* The girl who—?"

"Her mother."

"Oh God!" Beryl whispered. Then, "But she's married, too. What about—?"

"No one can come between us. Not now. She's my salvation, my talisman against the snake."

"*Snake?*" Beryl's eyes widened. He *was* mad!

"The reptile brain," he said, "digesting the cerebrum from within. It happened to Brouge."

Was this the theme of the book upstairs? And was he now relating it to himself? But he allowed her no time to follow his meaning. "And I'm just as necessary for her. Our coming together is the one thing which can make Arlette's death bearable for her. Surely you see that? Good coming out of grief?"

"I—don't know," she murmured, since he seemed to expect a reply.

"It's obvious enough." There was impatience in his voice, and from long habit, Beryl tried obligingly to understand.

"How does her husband feel about it?"

"That's immaterial. He must accept it, like the rest of us."

"Including me?"

"Yes. I'm sorry."

But incredibly, she was already accepting it—the explanation, if not, as yet, its outcome. For the change in him dated almost exactly from Arlette's disappearance—she'd already established that. Now, she could pinpoint it more finely. *Since the arrival of her parents.* But this long-lost-love story—was it true? Or had he, in his strange way, been overwhelmed by the Frenchwoman, and spun a fantasy round her? Surely Bernard, calm, self-possessed, almost, she thought blushingly, passionless, was incapable of such deep and lasting love? But perhaps, as he'd said himself, that was "immaterial." True or not, it was clear she herself was no longer wanted.

He was sitting in silence, with bowed head. She said almost sulkily, "So what happens now?"

"Cécile will accompany her daughter's body back to France, tidy up her affairs, and return here."

Beryl swallowed. "To this house, you mean?"

He looked at her in surprise. "It's my home."

"And mine!" she cried, tears starting to her eyes. "Have I no rights at all?"

"But you see," he said reasoningly, "I have to stay here because of my work, whereas you're free to start a new life wherever you choose. I'll make generous provision for you."

"I don't want 'generous provision,' I want my husband and my home!" She could feel the tears coursing down her cheeks, knew despairingly that now, when she most desperately needed to win him over, she must look her worst. He didn't speak, and after a moment, struggling for control, she said baldly, "You want me to get out. Is that it?"

Still no reply.

"And if I don't?" *The reason I killed my wife—* She shuddered involuntarily.

"The fault is mine, Beryl," he repeated patiently. "I accept that. You've been hurt, and I'm sorry. But Cécile and I suffered for *thirty years!* Surely we've earned some happiness?"

She said chokingly, "It's too bad you've had to put up with me so long. Don't worry, there'll be no more scenes. I'll pack a suitcase, and send a van for the rest of my things. Goodbye, Bernard."

She left the room with as much dignity as she could summon, and went upstairs. In a fog of misery she reached down a suitcase and almost randomly began to drop things into it. Could a marriage—a world—fall apart in two short weeks? When Arlette Picard disappeared, she'd thought she was happily married. If the girl hadn't died, her mother wouldn't have come, and nothing would have changed.

She heard the front door bang and moved to the window. As so many times in the past, she watched Bernard walk down the path, get into his car, and drive away. She couldn't believe it was the last time she'd do so.

She turned back to the case, closed it, and cast an unseeing glance round the room. Then she went downstairs. The two plates of fish were still on the table, the sauce congealing over them. Bile rose in her throat. Leaving them where they were, she went out to her own car, put the case on the back seat, then, as an afterthought, walked along the gravel behind the banks of conifers to the Marshbanks' house.

Claire came to the door, her face immediately concerned. "Beryl! Whatever is it?"

"I've come to say goodbye," Beryl said clearly. "I'm leaving Bernard. If that's the right way round."

Claire took her arm and led her inside. Beryl went unresistingly, allowed herself to be settled on the sofa, and accepted a small glass of brandy.

"Now, tell me what happened."

Calmly, she did so, omitting only Bernard's talking in his sleep. "I don't know whether to believe it or not," she finished. "It seems so improbable that I wondered if he'd just—deluded himself into thinking it was true. I mean, that poor husband! Surely she wouldn't leave him now, straight after their daughter's death?"

Claire said gently, "I think it is true, love. Daphne saw them together." And she repeated what Daphne'd told her.

"So that's it," Beryl said dully. "Well, it doesn't make much difference." She looked up, meeting Claire's eyes with a wan smile. "In fact, in a way it helps. When I learned that he'd never loved me, I thought it was my fault, that I'd failed him in some way. But I hadn't—he said so himself. He could have married the most beautiful, intelligent woman in the world, and it would have been the same. He was just so obsessed with this Cécile, he'd nothing left to give."

"What will you do?" Claire asked quietly.

"Go to my sister in Shillingham. She was widowed last year."

"But what about Melbray? You enjoy going there so much."

"Yes." Beryl paused. "I can't really think now. I'll stay with Marjorie for a while, till I decide what to do."

"Give me her phone number, then." Claire handed her a pad. "God, Beryl, I just can't take this in."

"How do you think I feel?" Beryl wrote down the number. "Keep an eye on Bernard for me, will you? He'll be alone for a week or two, till she gets back. Although a lot of things are explained, I still think he's ill." His comment about snakes returned to her, and, pushing it hastily from her mind, she rose to her feet. "I'd better go."

"Would you like me to come with you?"

"That's sweet of you, but I'll be all right. Sorry to let you down about Melbray. Sally Polsom would stand in, if you asked her. Oh, and I've just remembered: I promised Sarah I'd babysit tomorrow. Will you explain?"

"Of course. Oh, Beryl, I wish you weren't going."

"So do I." Beryl gave her a quick hug. "I'll phone you and we can meet for lunch. Now I really must go, before it starts to sink in."

"I'll ring this evening, to make sure you're all right."

Beryl nodded and walked back to her car. Claire stood at the door watching as she reversed into the road, raised a hand in farewell, and drove out of sight. Then she slowly closed it. Poor, poor Beryl.

Needing suddenly to hear Tom's voice, she went quickly to the telephone.

CHAPTER 12

Hannah stepped out of the shower and towelled herself vigorously. It had been a sticky, overcast day, with intermittent growls of thunder. On her return from school she'd flung open the windows, but the air was sluggish and no welcome breeze came in.

The bathroom lit momentarily as another crash rolled threateningly across the sky. Odd, Hannah thought, reaching for her clothes, how affected one was by weather. Problems which hung heavily in the rain dispersed with the sunshine, while storms held an underlying sense of menace and approaching climax.

She smiled to herself. Too much melodrama at an early age, she thought, hanging up the towel and emerging from the bathroom. A sulphury light filled the flat, and the first heavy raindrops splashed portentously on the sill beyond the sitting-room window. Hannah paused, looking down on the landscaped gardens. On the far side of the lawn was the wild patch, an area left uncultivated to attract insects and small animals. Beyond that again lay the protecting band of trees—oaks, elms, and chestnuts, all heavy now with summer foliage. Above their tops the sky hung loweringly as another peal, closer than the others, echoed overhead, setting some dogs barking.

"On such a night as this," Hannah thought, and shivered without knowing why. The rain, slow in reaching its decision, now began in earnest, falling in a heavy curtain behind which the garden shimmered as if seen through a waterfall. She moved back as it bounced on the inside sill, and reluctantly closed the window. At least she wasn't going out this evening. There was no likelihood of Charles ringing to suggest dinner.

And as the thought, half-rueful, half-relieved, formed in her head, the phone did ring. Hannah jumped, looking at it interrogatively. He'd said he'd try again, but surely not so soon? She lifted the phone. "Hello?"

"Mademoiselle James? I am sorry to disturb you." The voice spoke in quick, agitated French, introducing itself even as Hannah identified it. "This is Cécile Picard. I must thank you for your kind letter. My husband and I were deeply touched."

Hannah, mystified, murmured some reply. Her letter had called for no answer, least of all a telephoned one. "I hope you will forgive my troubling you," Madame continued, "but I have a problem—a serious one, I think—and I have no one else to turn to. You were so *sympathique* when we met, that I persuaded myself you might help me."

"If I can, of course."

"We must meet, mademoiselle. What I have to say cannot be discussed by telephone. May I see you this evening?"

Hannah hesitated, looking at the streaming windows. It was a fifty-minute drive to Steeple Bayliss. "Well, I—"

"Perhaps if I come to Shillingham, you will have dinner as my guest?"

Despite herself, Hannah said, "Surely it's easier if I—?"

"But no." The Frenchwoman was adamant. "I have checked the trains. If I catch the six-forty, I can be with you by seven-twenty. Would you be so kind as to book a table somewhere?"

Hannah said tentatively, "Your husband?"

"No, my husband knows nothing of this. I shall explain when I see you."

"Very well, madame. I'll meet you at the station. *A bientôt.*"

Hannah put the phone down and frowned. What problem could be urgent enough to bring the Frenchwoman twenty-seven miles on a wet evening, and without her husband's knowledge? She would have to wait and see. She opened the directory and flicked through it for the number of The King's Head. Better to go for the solid, old-fashioned ambiance of a hotel than a more ephemeral restaurant and, situated as it was on Gloucester Circus, it was only two minutes' drive from the station.

When the train came in, Hannah was waiting, protected from the weather by her full poplin raincoat and an umbrella. Madame looked as *chic* as ever in a riding mac with exaggerated collar and tightly pulled-in belt. She was pale, but she smiled as she shook Hannah's hand. "I am most grateful. I hope you had nothing planned?"

"Nothing," Hannah assured her, leading the way to the car. They spoke little as they drove down the busy, wet thoroughfare of Station Road and round to the hotel carpark. Sheltered by Hannah's umbrella, they hurried into the building, handing over their dripping coats and the umbrella to a solicitous cloakroom attendant.

"I booked the table for eight o'clock," Hannah said. "I thought perhaps you'd like a drink first?"

"Yes. Thank you."

They settled themselves in the cocktail lounge. A chromium bar ran down one side of the room, and there were plush bench seats along the other, behind a row of glass-topped tables. Hannah brought the drinks over.

"*Santé,*" she said, and Cécile Picard raised her glass. Hannah's eyes went over the attractive face with its high cheekbones and huge brown eyes, and the dark, silver-streaked hair which framed it. "I'm so very sorry about your daughter," she said.

"Thank you." Cécile toyed with her glass. "The police spoke with us today. It seems likely after all that it was an accident. I thank God for that. It hurts no less, but it is at least a clean pain. What tortured us was the thought that someone wished her harm. To know that was not so is comfort of a sort. You understand?"

Hannah nodded. "You have other children?" she asked gently.

"Oh yes. Another daughter and two sons. I miss them all so much." The French construction of the sentence gave it an added poignancy; not "I miss them," as in English, but, literally, "they are lacking to me." It seemed more expressive of what the woman felt.

"Tell me about them."

"Arlette is—was—the eldest. Then Xavier, who studies law. He will join his father's firm. Jean-Baptiste does his army service and Sylvie is still at school. They are so distressed about their sister and I should be with them, but I must stay until—" She spread her hands helplessly, and Hannah nodded.

"It won't be long now."

"No. I had thought I could manage, hold out until we return home, but now I don't think so."

"Hold out?"

"Forgive me, I should explain. But it is not easy, mademoiselle. It started so long ago. Thirty years. I was young—not yet twenty—and I fell deeply in love." She paused, still fingering her glass. "With a young Englishman. He was in Paris for a year, at the Sorbonne. It was all"—she gave a very Gallic shrug—"romantic, exciting, passionate, as perhaps only first love can be."

"Then he had to come home?"

"Not exactly. We quarrelled. I don't remember why. Nothing important, I'm sure. But I have a quick temper, and I indulged it to the full, enjoying the drama. 'It is over between us! Go and never return!' I expected him to respond, to shout back, then we would fall into each other's arms, more in love than ever. But he just stood there, looking pale and hurt, and I didn't know what to do. I ran out of the room, thinking he'd follow, but he did not. And the next day I heard he'd left Paris. I was—*désolée.* It seemed he hadn't loved me after all. I raged and cried for two solid days, then my mother, in despair, sent me to my aunt and cousins in Angers. And shortly afterwards I met my husband."

A waiter materialised in front of them. "Your table is ready, ladies, if you'd care to come through."

Hannah bit back her irritation. She couldn't see the relevance of what Madame was telling her, but the interruption had broken the flow. And in the dining-room there would be more distractions, studying the menu, ordering wine, the food being served. However, Cécile Picard, having finished her drink, was waiting for her. It was ten minutes later, when some of these distractions had been dealt with, that Hannah prompted, "And the young man? You never heard of him again?"

"Not for thirty years. Then I learned he'd caught the next boat back to France and searched for me everywhere. But my friends didn't know where I was, and my parents refused to tell him. They said I wanted no more to do with him. After all my tantrums, no doubt they believed that. And six months later, I married Gaston." Her face softened. "My husband is not a strong man, mademoiselle. He is gentle and sensitive, and his family is the centre of his life. He has grieved for Arlette even more than I, so much so it has made him ill. He has been forced to stay in his room ever since we arrived." She smiled sadly, meeting Hannah's eye. "You wonder why I bore you with this so long and ancient story. I will tell you. That young Englishman whom I loved so much, and who, despite what I thought, also loved me: his name was Bernard Warwick."

Hannah said blankly, "*Professor* Warwick? From the university?"

"*Exactement.*"

"But you must have known? Surely Arlette mentioned—?"

"Never. She seldom referred to him at all, and then only as '*le prof.*' And for his part, the name Picard meant nothing. He knew me as Cécile Devereux."

"So when did you both realise?"

"At the station, when he met our train."

"My God!" Hannah said softly. And David had been there. Had he noticed anything? "What did you do?"

"I was stunned. In the first seconds I took my lead from him, and since he continued to stare at me blankly, I gave no sign of recognition. He'd agreed to act as interpreter, but was too shocked to do so. He made his excuses and left, and Monsieur Webb found you to take his place."

"I see." She remembered David's anger at the professor's unaccountable behaviour. Unaccountable till now. "But you have seen him since?"

"Oh yes." There was a quiet bitterness in her voice. "Many times. He will not leave me alone. He—seems to think it is still thirty years ago."

"He still loves you?"

"Worse. He's convinced I still love him. Nothing I say will shake that belief. He maintains I'm just being loyal to my husband, whom he regards as weak. The day after our arrival, I went to the university. Gaston had a migraine, so I was alone. I see now that was a mistake, but to be truthful, I was glad of the chance to see Bernard privately. What woman is not curious about a former lover? I was totally unprepared for the—the tenderness and passion with which he greeted me. It was as though we'd been lovers the week before, and nothing had changed. As though, when he came back to look for me, I'd been waiting."

"But he must understand you're married now, and have your own life, your family—"

"He understands *nothing!*" Madame's small palm slapped the table, sloshing the wine in the glasses so that a drop spilt on the cloth. Absentmindedly she dabbed at it with her napkin.

"He phones repeatedly to the hotel. Somehow I've kept the calls from Gaston, who has often been in bed. I told you, mademoiselle, he is not strong; another shock on top of Arlette's death would be too much for him. It is for that reason alone that I excuse myself again and again to meet Bernard, to try to reason with him. But now a crisis has occurred."

"What's happened?"

Cécile waited till they'd been served with paper-thin slices of veal, tiny new potatoes, mangetouts, and broccoli. Then she said, as though there'd been no break in the conversation, "His wife has left him. He came to tell me this afternoon. He's becoming careless, not minding if we're seen together, and that is dangerous—for myself, for Gaston. He said he'd told her we are to marry, and she must go." Cécile looked up, holding Hannah's eyes. "And that was when, mademoiselle, for the first time, I was afraid. So I returned to my room and telephoned you."

"I see you're upset, madame, but why afraid?"

"Because he is no longer rational. He will accept nothing I say, brushes it aside and continues with his plans. Even to sending his wife away! It's—*bizarre.*" She sampled the veal appreciatively. "You know what I dreamt last night? That I was locked in a room with only a tiny, barred window. Through that window I could see a garden with a high gate and a wall all round it. And I could see Gaston and the children—Arlette was with them"—there was a break in her voice—"and they were trying to get in, to rescue me, but they could not. I woke with tears on my face."

"Then tell him," Hannah said. "Tell your husband the whole story. Then nothing Bernard says can harm you."

Slowly Cécile shook her head. "It is too late. I behaved foolishly at the beginning, not saying who Bernard was. But I did not think it important, God help me. Our thoughts were of Arlette, and that first evening as we reached our room, Gaston began to vomit. It was a story which needed careful telling. I was not capable, then, of embarking on it, nor he fit to listen. And as the days passed and I continued to reason with Bernard, it became impossible to speak. My silence gave it added importance. You see that?"

"Then go back to France, tomorrow, with your husband. Arlette will be flown back as soon as things are settled."

"No." Again Cécile shook her head. "I will not leave her alone, in a strange country. Look what happened last time."

It was illogical—what could harm Arlette now?—but Hannah understood.

"Then how can I help you?"

Cécile looked up and her face was suddenly haggard. In that moment, Hannah could imagine her as a very old woman. "I do not know. Perhaps you cannot. But I needed to tell someone, and no one else speaks French."

"He could be ordered to stop pestering you," Hannah said after a moment's thought.

"There's no time to go to court."

"Would you like someone to speak to him? Chief Inspector Webb, perhaps?"

"Ah!" Cécile smiled slightly. "Forgive me, I received the impression you know Monsieur Webb. Socially, that is."

Not much escaped the French, Hannah reflected. "Yes," she acknowledged.

"Then perhaps if you spoke with him, he might suggest something. You understand I want nothing public. I have no wish to humiliate Bernard, and it must not touch Gaston. He has enough to bear."

"I'll speak to Mr. Webb, certainly."

"This evening?"

"If he's available."

"I understand he is based in this town."

"Yes, and we live in the same block of flats."

"*Parfait.* I am sorry, mademoiselle, to burden you with my problems, but there is no one else. Now, let us speak of more pleasant topics. You own a school, I believe?"

"Not exactly," Hannah answered with a smile, and explained her position. The rest of the meal passed pleasantly enough in comparing the educational systems of England and France. But beneath the surface, Hannah's mind was still on the strange love story she'd heard. She hadn't met Professor Warwick; what kind of man could remain so passionately involved with a woman he hadn't seen or heard from in thirty years? And dismiss his wife, as though she were a servant he no longer required? More importantly, what would happen when his plans were thwarted, as they were bound to be?

Having determinedly put her troubles aside, Cécile Picard reverted to her vivacious self. Her face was mobile and expressive, given to quick, radiant smiles, and she used her hands repeatedly to convey her meaning. As a young girl, bubbling with *joie de vivre*, she must have been captivating.

Later, as they shook hands at the station, Hannah briefly reverted to the point of their meeting. "Try not to worry, madame. I'm sure things will work out for you. And I'll speak to Mr. Webb as soon as I get home."

As she came out of the forecourt, the thunderstorm, threatening for so long, finally broke. A deafening succession of crashes rolled across the sky, brilliantly illuminated by lightning, and the downpour of rain began with a roaring swoosh, rattling onto the paving stones and half-blinding her as she struggled to open the car door. The pavements of Station Road, quite busy when she drove up minutes before, were deserted as pedestrians huddled in shop doorways till the worst of the storm had passed. Slowly, her windscreen wipers struggling even on double-speed, Hannah drove along what seemed like a raging river-bed. The few cars she saw moving slowly along could have been empty, since the occupants were hidden behind the streaming windows. She felt alone and vulnerable, like a creature left behind by Noah's ark.

Above the noise of the car's engine and the rattling rain, another ear-numbing crash sounded. Grimly she continued along Duke Street and up the hill towards home. In the time it took her to garage the car and run into the building, her umbrella blew inside out and her hair was plastered to her head. It was with an atavistic sense of reaching shelter that she closed the front door behind her, leaning against it panting for a minute before, avoiding the lift in this electrical storm, she hurried up the stairs to her flat.

There, she changed out of her wet clothes, hung the poplin raincoat on the shower rail to drip in the bath, and rubbed the worst of the water off her hair. But she was not yet free to creep into bed, pulling the clothes over her head as she had as a child during thunderstorms. The evening was still not over; she had promised to contact David. Pulling the door shut behind her, she went up the stairs to his flat.

"Hannah! Come in!" Seeing her damp hair, he added, "You've surely not been out in this?"

"Oh, but I have."

"Then come and dry off. I'll light the gas fire—the rain's made it cooler. Can I get you a drink?"

"Coffee would be lovely, David. I've had enough alcohol this evening."

"Coming up," he said.

She knelt down on the rug before the instantly cheering fire, running her fingers through her hair and holding it out in layers to dry. Webb, coming back with the coffee, paused in the doorway, looking at the curve of her body and the fall of hair glowing in the firelight. Grimly he held down the surge of desire. She hadn't come for that, more was the pity.

"Here we are," he said briskly. "This'll warm you up."

She sat back on her heels, shaking her hair into place. Behind the curtained windows the lurid light gleamed again, and the electric one flickered in sympathy. Flickered, and went out.

"Hell's teeth!" Webb said under his breath. "That's all we need."

Hannah laughed. "We have the gas fire, and at least it gave you time to make coffee." She reached up for the mug he handed her, resettling herself on the rug. He sat in his own chair, watching her. The red light on their faces gave the illusion that they were huddled round a camp fire, safe from the raging storm. Hannah must have shared the thought, for she looked up at him, smiled, and said, "I have a tale to tell."

"Go ahead."

She sipped her coffee. "Before I do, is it true Arlette's death was accidental?"

"Strictly speaking, it's up to the adjourned inquest, but that'll be the verdict, yes."

"Are you glad?" She was thinking of the girl's mother. "Or, after all that work tracking down suspects, does it seem an anticlimax?"

"We weren't so much tracking down suspects as trying to establish how she died. That, we've done. The feeling should be relief rather than anticlimax."

She looked up. "Should be?"

"Unfortunately I don't feel it."

"Why not?"

"Because I've got this hunch that we're not at the end of it. Officially, it's all over bar the shouting, but I've got it fixed in my head that the girl's disappearance and death was only Act One of a continuing drama. I just wish to hell I knew what it was."

Hannah said quietly, "I may be able to help you there."

He leant forward, elbows resting on his knees. "How?"

"Can I ask you something first? When you went with Professor Warwick to meet the Picards, did you notice anything?"

His eyes had narrowed at the mention of Warwick, but he answered humorously, "You're asking that of a detective?"

She returned his smile. "Let me rephrase it: *what* did you notice?"

He considered, thinking back. "I'd only just met Warwick. He struck me as singularly unforthcoming. Not unhelpful—I don't mean that. That came later, as you know. Just—giving nothing away."

"And Madame? What was your first impression of her?"

Webb had a mental picture of her in the train doorway, holding on to the sides of it as her husband urged her down.

"That she regretted having come. She seemed in shock, as though she'd just realised what lay ahead."

"Did the professor say anything?"

"I heard him draw in his breath. I thought he was bracing himself, as I was." He added, "Why do you ask?"

"Because," Hannah said flatly, "they were lovers, thirty years ago in France."

"God in heaven!" Webb said softly. Then, "How do you know?"

"I've just had dinner with her. She phoned earlier and asked me to meet her."

"What possessed her to tell you that?"

"The best of reasons. She's afraid."

Webb stiffened. "Of what?"

"Of him. He won't accept that thirty years have passed. He's convinced she's still in love with him, as he is with her, and that they're about to marry. He's even sent his wife packing."

"He's *what?*" He didn't wait for her to repeat it. He stood up abruptly, his face going into the shadows above the firelight. "*That's* it! That's what's been worrying me all along. Bernard Warwick. I said before he was a walking time-bomb. Now he hasn't even got his wife to calm him, and as the time approaches for the Picards to leave, he'll become more and more desperate." He paused. "It seems I was right. The girl's death was only the prelude, the catalyst that brought them back together."

Hannah looked up at him, the fire warm on her throat. "What can you do?"

"We'll have to move carefully. He hasn't committed an offence."

"Nuisance value? He keeps pestering her and she's humoured him to keep him away from her husband." She explained Monsieur Picard's state of health.

Webb sat down again, clasping his hands together and flexing his fingers as he reviewed the possibilities. "Simon might be our best bet in the first place."

"Simon?"

"DC Marshbanks. His parents live next door to the Warwicks. I'll send him over tomorrow, to scout out the land. Another alternative is to move the Picards out, fast."

"They won't go without the body. In any case, in his present state of mind he'd only follow them. It would be easy enough to find out their address—the hotel register, for a start. He may have already checked, he was there today." She frowned, added tentatively, "Perhaps we're over-reacting? He doesn't mean them any harm, after all. Quite the reverse."

"He doesn't mean *her* any," Webb corrected grimly. "We don't know how he regards Picard."

"If he attacked her husband, it would hardly endear him to her, would it? He'd be aware of that."

"I suppose so. And if, as you say, Picard never leaves his room, he should be safe enough. All the same, we might put someone inconspicuous in the lobby, to watch the comings and goings. I'll have a word with Chris Ledbetter in the morning."

Outside, the storm still raged. Hannah got to her feet, felt her way to the window, and drew back the curtains. Webb's flat, unlike hers, was at the front of the building, with a view down the long hill to the town. There were no street or house lights—a main cable must be down. The only illumination came from the jagged zigzags which periodically tore the sky open. She heard David come up behind her, tensed for a moment, then relaxed. After all, why had she refused Charles? He stood beside her, a hand lightly on her shoulder.

"It shows how dependent we are on the flick of a switch. One blow from Mother Nature and we're helpless. We can't see, can't cook, in many cases can't even keep warm. And such modern refinements as TV, freezers, and computers are completely useless. It brings us down to size, doesn't it?"

She nodded, but only absently. She was acutely aware of his closeness, even more conscious of the time-lapse since they had last been together. He bent his head and his lips brushed across her hair. "Those stairs down to your flat, for instance. It would be madness to tackle them in the dark. I couldn't accept the responsibility."

"So what do you suggest?" she asked softly, a smile sounding in her voice.

"I'll give you three guesses." He turned her gently to face him, still hardly daring to believe that, after all, he was to be given another chance.

Hannah let her breath out in a sigh. "In that case, Chief Inspector, I'll be happy to accept police protection."

The next crash of thunder broke directly overhead, but neither of them heard it.

CHAPTER 13

"So I said to her, 'Well, I've told you before, Mrs. Davis,' I said, 'you're too soft with her. A good old-fashioned smack on the bottom, that's what she needs.' Told her straight, I did. If you ask me, it's what half the kids these days need. No discipline, no one to tell them what's right and wrong. A crying shame, I call it."

Claire nodded absently, resigned to the continuing saga of Sandra Davis. It was time she left for Melbray, but she was worried about Bernard. His car was still in the drive, so he'd not gone to work. Should she go to see if he was all right? She'd promised Beryl to keep an eye on him. And how was Beryl, waking this morning to a bleak new existence?

"—Rick Parker. 'Well,' I said to her, 'I wouldn't trust that lad with my budgie. Eyes too close together.' I could see that upset her, but I have to speak my mind. You must be cruel to be kind, sometimes. I wonder if they've found out who murdered that French girl," Edna continued without pause, and Claire, groping her way through the verbiage, almost missed the reference.

"It's not definite she *was* murdered," she said mildly.

Edna sniffed derisively. "Course she was murdered, Miss Claire, and no wonder, neither, the way she carried on. I said as much to Mrs. Davis. 'You tell your Sandra to watch her step,' I said, 'or she might finish up the same way.' " Edna pushed her glasses up, nodding to herself with grim satisfaction. "Well, I can't stand here chatting all day," she added accusingly, "I've my bedrooms to see to." And to Claire's relief she lifted the vacuum cleaner and stumped from the room.

Claire followed her as far as the hall and turned into the sitting-room, where she glanced undecidedly at the clock. She really ought to be going—she'd promised to stand in for Daphne. Sally Polsom was holding the fort, but she couldn't do so indefinitely. The trouble, as Claire admitted to herself, was that she felt apprehensive about approaching Bernard. But if she didn't, she'd be worrying about him all day. Just a very brief call, then, to make sure—

A familiar rattling and roaring outside sent her hurrying to the window, and her face lit up. *The Hesperus,* battered but unbowed, had turned into the driveway and Simon was getting out. Claire ran to the front door.

"Darling! What a lovely surprise! Have you a day's leave?"

He returned her hug, glancing towards the house next door. "Let's go inside, Mum, and I'll explain."

"Nothing's wrong, is it?" Claire asked in quick alarm.

"No, no. Everything's OK."

As they went through the front door, Edna appeared at the top of the stairs. "Nice to see you, Master Simon," she called down. "We was just wondering if you've caught that killer yet."

"What killer would that be, Edna?"

"The one that did the French girl in, of course." Even Edna, Claire reflected, would not have been so tactless had she known of Simon's connection with Arlette.

He was answering gravely, "She fell, Edna. No one was near her when she died."

"Is that true, Simon?" Claire cut in. "Well, thank God. It doesn't alter the fact that she's dead, but at least no one's under suspicion."

Simon closed the sitting-room door. "This isn't leave, Mum," he said quietly, "it's semi-official. About Bernard."

Claire went cold. "What about him?"

"You know Beryl's gone?"

"Yes, but how do *you?*"

"And that Bernard and Arlette's mother knew each other years ago?" Claire nodded. It might be her son who was speaking, but he was doing so in an official capacity, representing the law of the land, and she felt oddly ambivalent.

"Well, apparently he's been making a nuisance of himself, ringing her up all the time and so on."

"But they're going to get married," Claire protested. "That's why Beryl left."

"He told her that?"

"You mean it's not true?" She was staring at him in bewilderment.

"Not a word of it. She's no intention of leaving her husband."

"Then why did he send Beryl away?"

Simon shrugged. He was standing with his back to the empty grate. He looked young and earnest and much as he'd always done, but there was a patina of authority laid over his youth that was at the same time touching and impressive. "How does he seem? In himself?"

"Distinctly odd," Claire said with a shiver, and it was to the policeman that she replied. She wouldn't have dreamed of discussing her friends with her children. "I woke one night about a week ago and went to the window for some air. Bernard was out in his garden, standing quite still. I watched him for several minutes, and he never moved. And when they came to dinner the next evening, his behaviour was most peculiar. Beryl was very worried about him."

"That would be when he'd just met Madame."

"Of course. I never thought of that."

"What exactly did Beryl say before she left?"

"That Bernard was marrying Madame Picard."

"Did it come as a shock?"

"Well yes, though not totally out of the blue. She'd told me earlier that he didn't love her."

"When was that? Recently?"

"Yes, last Sunday. I called round when I got back from Melbray." She hesitated, then unwillingly related the episode of the breadknife. To her relief, Simon didn't comment on it.

"But the bit about Madame Picard must have surprised you," he said.

"Well, actually, no. Daphne Farlow saw them together. I hadn't mentioned it to Beryl, though."

"Was she very upset about going?"

"I think she'd accepted it. She said Bernard seemed in a daze and didn't hear when she spoke to him. She thinks he's mentally ill."

"But she hasn't called anyone in?"

"He wouldn't let her."

"I see his car's there. Have you anything I could take round, as an excuse for calling? A cake, or something like that?"

"There are some drop-scones I made yesterday. I know he likes them."

"Perfect."

She said tentatively, "Don't—harass him, darling. I promised Beryl I'd keep an eye on him."

"Don't worry, Mum, I'll go very carefully."

Bernard saw Simon's wreck of a car arrive next door. The long arm of the law, he thought, and laughed aloud. He had woken that morning with a feeling of elation. He was free! Beryl had gone with the minimum of fuss and Cécile, his love, was within his reach at last.

He'd no lectures that day, and had decided to work at home. There'd be no interruptions with unwanted tea or coffee—but no lunch, either. He remembered the unappetising plates he'd found last night, and wrinkled his nose in distaste. Yet if cold fish was the only mess left at the break-up of a marriage, he'd no cause to complain.

But, with the day stretching ahead of him, he was unable to settle. He yearned for Cécile, ached to hold her again. Surely he'd been patient long enough? He accepted her reluctance to hurt Picard, but he was himself entitled to some consideration. Perhaps he should go to the hotel again, persuade her to bring matters to a head.

As he reached that decision the doorbell chimed, and he answered it to find young Simon on the step. Alarm bells rang in his head. Never, in the four years he'd lived here, had the boy called before. What brought him now? The bag of scones he self-consciously held didn't deceive Bernard for a moment. He must watch his words, let nothing slip. Smiling, he held the door wide.

"Simon! What a delightful surprise! Come in, boy, come in. Have you got the day off?"

"Not entirely. I'm on my way to Maybury Street, but I took the chance to call on Mum. She sent these scones, by the way." He held them out awkwardly. "How are you, Bernard?" He always felt embarrassed addressing the austere professor by his first name, but Beryl had pressed these on himself and Sarah when the Warwicks first arrived.

"Never better, my boy, never better." He sobered briefly. "That's very thoughtful of your mother. You'll have heard that Beryl's left me?"

"Yes. I'm sorry."

"Oh, don't be, don't be. We were always ill-matched, I'm afraid. This had been brewing for a long time; we're better apart. But we mustn't stand talking in the hall. Come to the kitchen and I'll make some coffee."

"I don't want to disturb you," Simon said warily, following him as requested. He was baffled by Bernard's affability and unsure what he was supposed to be looking for. The governor had been vague—"Play it by ear and report back," he'd said.

He asked tentatively, "Will you stay on here alone?"

Bernard smiled, plugging in the coffee machine. "I shan't be alone, Simon. I'll be marrying again, as soon as circumstances allow. Have you met Madame Picard?"

"I—er, no, I haven't. But I knew her daughter."

"Ah yes. A very sad business." But it had brought him Cécile. Because of that, he found it hard to regret Arlette's death. He mourned her only on Cécile's behalf.

"You'll be marrying Madame Picard?" Simon pursued valiantly.

"Yes, indeed. We should have done so years ago, when we were young."

"So she's getting a divorce too?"

Bernard frowned fleetingly. "Of course."

Simon swallowed hard. "She has agreed to marry you?"

He feared a strong reprimand at his persistence, but Bernard laughed. "Never been in love, Simon? If you had, you wouldn't need to ask such questions."

Which was no answer at all. Yet short of downright rudeness, he could pursue it no further. DI Ledbetter could take it from here.

Having done his duty to the best of his ability, Simon thankfully slipped off his mental uniform and relaxed. Bernard noted the change, and smiled to himself. Did they suspect him of doing away with Beryl? Think her body might be buried in the garden? If so, they were welcome to look. He'd considered killing her, true, but only academically. He couldn't be tried for that. And in the event she'd gone surprisingly quietly. Gaston Picard was the only obstacle that remained.

When Simon left, Bernard waited for a while, keeping an eye on the frightful green car. Ten minutes later, the boy and his mother emerged from the next-door house, got into their respective cars, and drove away. As soon as they were out of sight, Bernard did likewise, and made his way to The White Swan carpark. For no other reason than it was the nearest entrance, he went into the building the back way, walked past the kitchens and deserted bars, and emerged in the foyer by the reception desk.

Alerted by Simon's visit, he spotted the plain-clothes man at once. He was facing away from Bernard, towards the lifts and staircase, and Bernard himself had not been seen. He moved swiftly back into the corridor to review the position. Whoever the man was watching for, it was clear that no one could go either up or downstairs without being seen. Except, thought Bernard, with growing excitement, by the back stairs which he'd just passed. He lingered a while longer, frustrated by being so near Cécile but unable to approach her discreetly. And as he hesitated, one of the lift doors opened and Cécile herself stepped out.

Now—would she be followed? Bernard waited with held breath, but the man remained engrossed in his newspaper, and Cécile, apparently unaware of him, walked purposefully across the foyer and through the swing doors to the street. Bernard was tempted to follow her, but a more daring plan was taking shape. He could approach Picard direct, discover how far Cécile had prepared him for their imminent parting.

Careful not to attract the detective's attention, he slipped back the way he had come and crossed the road to a phone box. His request to speak to Monsieur Picard was not questioned; had it been, he'd have identified himself as a police officer. The bell sounded for several minutes before the phone was lifted.

"*Allo?*"

Bernard's fingers were slippery with sweat. "Good day, monsieur," he said in French. "This is Professor Warwick. We met at the railway station."

"Of course. Good day, Professor."

"I wonder if it would be possible for us to meet?"

"We should be honoured. When my wife returns, I—"

"No, monsieur, I wish to see you alone." And as the man hesitated, weak fool that he was, Bernard added, "It concerns your daughter."

"Arlette?" The voice cracked.

"Arlette. Will you see me?"

"But naturally. You must forgive me, *monsieur le professeur*, I do not know the town. I—"

Bernard said rapidly, "I suggest you leave by the back stairs. This is important. Someone is watching the hallway."

"Someone—? I don't understand."

"I'll explain when I see you. Go down the back stairs and

out through the door at the foot of them. It leads to the hotel carpark. I'll meet you there."

"Very well. At what time do you wish to see me?"

"Now. Immediately." There was no knowing how long Cécile would be.

"*D'accord,*" Picard said again. "I will come straight down."

Bernard pushed his way out of the kiosk and ran back to his car. Moments later, the back door of the hotel opened and Picard emerged, looking vaguely about him. Bernard went to meet him. The man looked thin and frail, the fine bone structure very near the surface of the skin. His large, poet's eyes were mournful, with purple shadows beneath them, but he gave a perfunctory smile of recognition and took the hand Bernard held out. Bernard settled him in the car as swiftly as possible and, driving rapidly out of the carpark, turned onto Gloucester Road.

"You wish to speak of Arlette, monsieur?"

"Actually, no. It is Cécile we must discuss."

"Cécile?" His head turned in surprise at the familiarity. "You speak of my wife?"

"That's correct." Bernard was concentrating on getting out of town. He did not wish to be seen by anyone who knew him. "Has she mentioned me?"

"Why should she?" There was a coolness in Picard's voice. He didn't care to have his wife's name bandied about.

"Because we are old friends, she and I."

There was a silence while the Frenchman digested this surprising piece of information. Then he said stiffly, "I regret I cannot accept that."

So she'd said nothing. Bernard felt a spurt of irritation. Really, she was over-protective. It was as well he'd taken matters into his own hands; the time for procrastination was past.

"I assure you it's true. In fact, we were more than friends, we were lovers."

Picard jerked as though stung. "Monsieur, I protest. You

lied to bring me here, now you slander my wife. I demand you return to the hotel."

"She'll confirm it, if you ask her. She's been trying to spare you pain."

"You presume too much. Kindly stop the car. I will find my own way back."

"We must talk, my friend. There's been too much secrecy. Cécile and I are to be married."

The man stared fixedly at Bernard's profile. "You are mad!" he whispered. "You don't know what you're saying."

Bernard had turned off the road and was following that taken, ten days earlier, by Nigel Morgan. It was not by chance. He didn't reply till he had reached the nearest point to the place where Arlette had fallen. Then he switched off the ignition and turned to his distraught passenger.

"Now, monsieur," he said softly, "we shall have our discussion."

So this was Dave's blue-eyed boy. Or brown-eyed, to be accurate. A smart lad, Ledbetter conceded to himself, alert and capable, by the look of him. He'd delivered his report clearly and concisely, standing to attention with his eyes fixed on the wall above Ledbetter's head. Now he awaited a reaction and possible further orders.

"Your mother hadn't told you she knew of the connection?"

"No, sir, but I haven't seen her for some time. It's not a thing she'd mention on the phone."

"Did Warwick strike you this morning as unbalanced?"

"Not at all. He seemed happier than I've ever seen him."

"But he's genuinely convinced this marriage will take place?"

"No doubt of that, sir."

Ledbetter tapped his pen on his desk. "So who do we believe? A respected English professor, or a hysterical Frenchwoman who's just lost her daughter? She could be playing the men off against each other. At her age, she might need to feel she's still attractive."

A sexist remark if ever he'd heard one. "Or he might," Simon said, straight-faced.

Ledbetter laughed at the implied rebuke. "You have a point, young Marshbanks. Well, we've got a face in the hotel lobby, checking everyone going up or down, and another outside, who's phoned to report following Madame to a hairdresser's. No one tried to approach her, and she'll be discreetly escorted back again."

"Have you anyone watching the professor, sir?"

"No point. As long as he keeps away from those two, he can do what the hell he likes."

"And phone calls?"

"That's a bit more tricky. We don't want to make a song and dance by having them intercepted. In any case, she can always hang up. It's only a question of marking time till they leave the country, and the clearance should come through any day now."

"What if he follows them?"

"That, I'm glad to say, will be a French pigeon."

"Anything else you'd like me to do, sir?"

Ledbetter shook his head. "Warwick had to be sussed out informally, and you were the obvious choice, but we'll take it from there. Thanks for your help, Constable."

"Sorry I'm so late, Sally. It's been rather a fraught morning."

"That's all right. Things are pretty quiet here." Sally eyed Claire with interest. "You *do* look a bit ragged, old thing. What's up?"

There seemed little point in secrecy. It would be out soon enough. "It's Beryl. She's left Bernard."

Sally stared at her open-mouthed. "*Beryl* has left *Bernard?* But she thought the sun shone out of him!"

Claire sighed and sat down at her desk. "It was pretty much at his request."

"Ah. That's different. A cold fish, he looks to me. I can't think what she ever saw in him."

"Nevertheless, she's very upset."

"She would be, poor love. And you being on the doorstep, so to speak, landed right in it. Poor old Claire, no wonder you're rough round the edges."

"I promised to keep an eye on him. I was steeling myself to call round when Simon arrived, and I cravenly let him go instead. He came back with the report that he's all smiles and happy as a sandboy."

"More than she is, I'll bet. Don't waste your sympathy on him."

"Not sympathy, exactly." But Claire couldn't elaborate. Sally, while goodhearted, was known to gossip.

"You think she's gone for good?"

Claire shrugged. "Who knows?"

"What I mean is, I'm quite happy to help out on a long-term basis. Till she sorts herself out, at least."

"That's kind of you, Sally," Claire said gratefully. "Thanks."

Bernard was becoming increasingly agitated and the snakes, which had been dormant this morning, were slithering round in his head. He could hear their dry rustling with his inner ear, and shook his head irritably to clear it. The pig-headed Frenchman was stronger-minded than he looked, and despite half an hour's reasoning and explaining, refused even to contemplate the idea of divorce. "I shall not believe a word till I hear it from my wife," he kept repeating.

He'd been shaken, though, when Bernard cited the times of his meetings with Cécile. For the last ten minutes he'd not spoken at all, and Bernard stared at him in exasperation. Couldn't the fool see he *had* to have Cécile, not only because he loved her, but for the sake of sanity. She alone could steer him across the seething snakepit of his mind.

Abruptly, he opened the car door and got out. "We're just

by the place where Arlette fell," he said. "Would you like to see it?"

A tremor went over the thin, aesthetic face. "That is true? You're sure?"

"I'm sure. Everyone in town knows the spot. I thought you might like to say a prayer there."

Picard looked at him disbelievingly, but he eased himself out of the car. Slowly, with Bernard impatiently curbing his pace to match his companion's, they began to climb over the rough ground. Last night's storm had left the day newly minted, the sky clear-washed and brilliant blue. The sun hadn't reached this side of the hill, and it was still wet underfoot.

"You knew my daughter?" Picard asked suddenly.

"Only by sight. I'd no idea who she was."

The Frenchman, shying from the implied reference to his wife, brought the conversation back to Arlette. "Was she happy here, do you think?"

"Very, from what people say. She was a popular girl."

"Yes," her father answered softly, "she had the gift, from a child, of making people love her. So full of life always." He reached for a handkerchief and dabbed his eyes. "It is impossible to accept."

Bernard felt a wave of pity. "You have other children, though; they'll be a comfort to you. I've no one but Cécile."

Picard said crisply, "You should not have dismissed your wife. I assure you, monsieur, you shall not have mine."

"Look, I know it's hard, coming so soon after Arlette's death. But we're *meant* for each other, Cécile and I. Except for a misunderstanding, we'd have been together all these years." He hesitated. "Surely she mentioned me, when you first met?"

"She said there'd been someone," Picard admitted unwillingly, "an Englishman. But she'd found after all he hadn't loved her."

"That," Bernard said tensely, "was the misunderstanding.

There hasn't been a day in thirty years when I've not longed for her. And it's been the same for her."

"You are mistaken, monsieur. Our marriage has been entirely happy, until this tragedy."

"Then you've much to be thankful for, is that not so? Now it's our turn for happiness."

Picard shook his head helplessly and continued the climb. He moved only slowly, with frequent pauses for breath, and the walk was taking longer than Bernard had expected. Not that there was any hurry; it would be late afternoon before Claire returned from Melbray, and with his driveway hidden from the road, no one else would notice if his car was missing. And as the thought came to him, he realised what he'd subconsciously been planning all along, holding as a last resort if all else failed.

The hope of amicable divorce, he saw now, was pure fantasy, and in accepting that, he faced a new danger. For Cécile was tender-hearted and, if her husband broke down and begged her to stay, she was quite capable of doing so. Which was a risk Bernard couldn't take. Not now. Not this time.

On the other hand, if Picard could be convinced that she was leaving him, he might well attempt suicide. And what better place than the spot where his beloved daughter had died? Systematically, Bernard began to play on Picard's raw emotions.

"She must have climbed up here, just where we are now. I wonder if her lover was with her."

"My daughter had no lovers," Picard said tremulously. "She was a virtuous girl."

"She'd come with a man, anyway; the police have established that. And why else would he bring her out here?" The man's eyes were full of tears. So far, so good.

But Gaston, exhausted and distressed though he was, continued to defend his daughter. "Then it was because she refused him that he drove off without her."

"Perhaps," Bernard conceded indifferently. "But you can picture her, can't you, desperate to get back to town, and with no means of transport? She must have stood just here, seen that busy road, and decided to climb down and hitch a lift. Isn't that how the police think it happened?"

He glanced sideways, saw the tears raining down the Frenchman's face. He was suffering, all right. If he didn't take the obvious way out of his misery, Bernard must do it for him. It would be a kindness, really, like stamping on an injured butterfly. The *coup de grâce.*

"This, monsieur," he repeated softly, "is where your daughter spent her last minutes on earth. Can you feel her close? Perhaps she's lonely, out there in infinity. Perhaps she calls to you to join her." He lowered his voice, mesmerised by his own words. "It would end all your sufferings, *n'est-ce pas, mon ami?* And after the initial shock, Cécile would be free. I'd take good care of her, I promise you, and of your other children. You need have no fear."

"*Que vous êtes diabolique!*" Picard's voice was clogged with tears. "*Satan lui-même.*"

"If I were to drive off and leave you, what then? Would you, too, attempt to climb down the hillside? You are weaker than your daughter, monsieur. If she slipped and fell, what chance have you? Shall we find out?"

Picard turned a startled face towards him and saw, too late, the intent in Bernard's deranged eyes. He gave a choked cry, flailed his arms wildly for a moment, and then, as Bernard pushed firmly against his chest, went over the edge with a nerve-chilling scream. The echo of it resounded in Bernard's ears for several minutes after the sound had died. Cautiously, he looked over the edge. Sure enough, Picard lay on his back on the rocky ledge where his daughter had died. On the gorse bush, the first, yellow buds were starting to appear.

Bernard turned and made his way, alone, back to his car.

CHAPTER 14

The hotel receptionist smiled brightly. "Good afternoon. Can I help you?"

"If you please." The woman in front of her spoke slowly, with a strong accent. "Could you tell me, please, if my husband left a message for me?"

"What is your room number, madam?"

Cécile told her, and watched as she turned and scanned the relevant pigeon-hole. "No, madam, there's no message."

Cécile nodded her thanks and turned away. There'd been no sign of Gaston when she returned from the hairdresser's, though she'd looked in all the public rooms. He'd been feeling better when she left, so perhaps he'd followed her suggestion of a stroll to the river. That would be why he'd not bothered with a note. But it was now after one, and people were going in for lunch.

She turned back to the desk. "Do you know at what hour he went out?"

The girl looked surprised. "I'm afraid I don't know your husband, madam."

A large man, who had been sitting in the foyer most of the morning, detached himself from his chair and came across, ostensibly to flick through the rack of postcards farther down the desk.

"He is blond, and tall—" Cécile faltered.

"Perhaps this gentleman can help you."

"If I can, ma'am." Detective Constable Rowley was uneasy. He'd caught only a snatch of the stilted conversation, but hadn't liked what he heard.

Taking pity on Cécile's lack of English, the receptionist

explained, "This lady wonders if anyone saw her husband go out, and if so, at what time."

"Go out?" Rowley's startled exclamation surprised both his hearers. "He can't have done. I've been here all morning."

"You know my husband, monsieur?"

Rowley back-pedalled. "I heard your description, ma'am. Tall, fair gentleman, you said. No one like that has gone out this morning."

Cécile said with a touch of impatience, "Monsieur, there is no question that my husband went out. I require only to know when."

Since no one seemed able to help her, she walked through the swing doors and stood on the pavement looking up and down the street. Suppose he'd gone farther than he realised, and become lost. Would he be able to ask directions, or understand any he was given? Would he even remember the name of the hotel? But surely if he said "by the river"—even "*près de la rivière*"—an English person should understand. But suppose, instead, he'd been taken ill somewhere? Rushed off to hospital? *Oh, Gaston, reviens, je t'implore!*

John Rowley had shut himself inside the telephone booth in the foyer. "Guv, I swear he couldn't have got past me."

Ledbetter pursed his lips. "There's been no sign of Warwick?"

"Not a whisker. Anyway, if Picard *had* gone out, Bob would have seen him."

"Not if he was tailing Madame to the hairdresser's. Well, never mind, John, it's not a matter of life and death. We're only trying to stop the professor from annoying them. If we slipped up, we'll just apologise and put it down to human error."

"Not *my* human error," Rowley repeated stubbornly. "I'd stake my life on it. He never went through those doors."

"OK, John, no sweat. But let me know when he gets back."

Rowley had put the phone down before he realised the DI

had had the last word in more than one way. Swearing softly, he too went out onto the street. There was no sign of Bob Jeffries; he'd have followed Madame again.

On an impulse, Rowley went back inside and took the lift to the third floor. As he'd guessed, the door to room 313 was on the latch. He stepped inside and looked quickly round, not sure how long he had before the woman came back. Two suitcases were on the luggage stand, a row of bottles and jars on the dressing table. The rest of the room was neat and impersonal. A breath of expensive scent reached him on the draught of his movement.

Feeling foolish, he opened the wardrobe door, briefly scanning the few dresses that hung there. Then he pushed open the bathroom door and looked inside. It, too, was clean and empty. What had he expected? Did he really think she might have over-looked her husband's presence? Yet he was so sure Picard hadn't appeared in the lobby. Well, he'd been proved wrong, damn it. He resented the slur on his professionalism, even though the governor hadn't seemed too worried.

There was nothing here for him. After a cautious look up and down the corridor, he slid out of the door, leaving it as he'd found it, and went back to his post in the lobby, guarding the now empty stable.

At Divisional Headquarters in Shillingham, Chief Inspector Webb sat glumly at his desk, contemplating the mound of paperwork which had built up in his absence.

"Can't have it all ways, Dave!" Crombie remarked, grinning. "You said you wanted some excitement, and you got it, but the papers haven't just melted away."

Webb grunted, thinking back to the day the case started, and his frustration at seeing Hannah with Frobisher. At least, thank God, that last emotion hadn't been waiting here to reclaim him. Last night—but if he started thinking of that, the paperwork would never get done. The phone on his desk rang, and, glad of the distraction, he lifted it. "DCI Webb."

"Hello, Dave. Chris here. Just ringing to say your lad's

been in to report on Warwick. The professor's fine, apparently, all smiles and not a worry in sight. But he's convinced he's going to be a bridegroom."

"You call that fine? He must be off his rocker."

"Oh, come on, let that bee out of your bonnet. The case is *over,* for Pete's sake. She must just have been playing him along."

"Why should she do that?"

"Who knows? Perhaps for leaving her all those years ago. He'll get a nasty shock, but he's not the first one, and he won't be the last, so why get our knickers in a twist? Anyway, we're keeping an eye on the Picards—or trying to. The husband seems to have given us the slip."

"*What?*" Webb came to his feet, and Crombie looked up from his papers.

"Gone walkabout in the sunshine. So what? Warwick's not been near him."

"How do you know?"

"We've a bloke planted in the hall."

"Then why the hell didn't he see Picard?"

"Hold on, now, Dave. I don't know. It was a slip-up, though he won't admit it. Good cop, too, John Rowley."

"If he didn't see Picard," Webb said evenly, controlling his temper, "he might have missed Warwick, as well."

"My God, Dave, you're really neurotic about that man! I *told* you—"

"Humour me. Send someone round *now,* to the university and to Warwick's house. Find out where he is and how long he's been there, and ring me back."

"Yes, sir."

Webb consciously eased his grip on the receiver. "Sorry, Chris, but I have bad vibes about this guy."

"OK, OK, I'll send two cars to check on him."

"And you'll ring me back?"

"I'll ring you back."

Webb sat down slowly and looked at his watch. It was two

o'clock. Across the room, Crombie, deciding questions would be unwise, returned to his work.

It was important, Bernard felt, to review the position in detail, check there was nothing he'd over-looked. Though he longed to phone Cécile, he must contain himself. Gaston's death would be a shock to her. Still, father and daughter could have a double funeral, which would be preferable to drawing out the agony. He accepted there would be agony, for the remaining children, at least. But it would all be seen to decorously and with due ceremony. As to his divorce, these things could be put through quickly now and he didn't foresee any hold-up. So in—what?—three months?—they'd be free to marry. After thirty years, he could wait another three months.

In the meantime, he must plan what to tell her, and at what stage. Thinking of Gaston, the snakes moved restlessly, but they no longer distressed him. He had the means of their destruction at hand. Love conquers all, he thought fatuously, even serpents. Poor, poor Brouge! How different his life might have been, had Jeanne Collière come back into it. Perhaps he should add an addendum to his *Life.* He'd not realised, when he wrote the book, the full significance of the snakes and the reptilian brain.

A police car drew up at the gate, and he frowned, annoyed at the interruption. Were they still looking for Beryl? Perhaps they'd come to dig up the garden. She was probably at Marjorie's, but he wasn't obliged to tell them that. If they wanted to search for a hidden grave, they were welcome. He opened the door, staring woodenly at the two young men on the step. Not Simon Marshbanks, this time. Ye gods, the house was becoming police-ridden.

"Sorry to trouble you, sir," said the spokesman, producing his card. "Could you tell us what your movements have been today?"

"I could, certainly, but why should I?"

The young man flushed. "Routine inquiries, sir."

"Don't treat me like an idiot, officer. Constable Marshbanks has already been round. However, since it interests you, I've been home all day. I *was* hoping to work uninterrupted."

"Would it be all right if we stepped inside for a moment?"

"You have a search warrant?"

"No, sir, nothing like that. Just a quick look round, if it's all right. It won't take a minute."

Bernard sighed heavily. "Very well, come in."

He stood in the hall while the two officers went swiftly over the house, opening doors and cupboards and looking under beds, by the sound of it. Did they think he'd hidden her indoors? Only as they met again in the hall, exchanging a quick shake of the head, did he realise it was not Beryl who interested them.

"Do you know Mr. Gaston Picard, sir?"

The unexpectedness of the question shook him, but his habitual mask gave no hint of his alarm. "I met him last week, when he arrived in this country."

"Have you seen him since, sir?"

"I have not. I heard he was confined to his room." He paused, added with finely judged amusement, "Why, have you lost him?"

"And you haven't left the house at all today?"

"No, Constable, I have not. Do you want it in writing?"

"Sorry to have troubled you, sir," the young man said stolidly, and they both took their leave. Bernard stood looking after them, smiling to himself as a casual hand patted the bonnet of the car as they passed it in the drive. The engine had had time to cool down, and in any case the strong sun pouring down on it would account for any residual warmth. Still, why should they think he knew anything about Gaston?

Then he remembered. He'd spoken to Simon that morning of his impending marriage. That had been less than wise. He really must be more careful about confiding in people, especially the gentlemen, either actually or metaphorically, in blue.

For the third time that afternoon, Cécile returned to the hotel to find no news of Gaston. She was hot and sticky, as much from her growing panic as the heat of the day and her incessant searching. On this occasion she paused long enough to bathe her blistered feet and change her blouse.

Then, reining her stampeding thoughts, she tried to be objective. Was there anything she'd missed? Anything which, with hindsight, could seem significant?

She had left Gaston at five past eleven, in time for her eleven-fifteen appointment. She conjured him up in her mind, sitting in that chair, the cushion of which still bore the imprint of his body. Impulsively she moved to it, laying her hand in the indentation. Oh God, where was he? Why hadn't he left a note, telling her where to find him? She felt wretchedly alone, not knowing how officialdom operated here. She could try the hospitals, but how to discover which and where they were?

Suppose—her breath almost choked her—suppose, suddenly becoming faint as he walked by the river, he had stumbled and fallen into the water, and no one had seen him?

She put her hands to her burning cheeks. She shouldn't have left him! Yet he'd been all right all those other times, when she'd had to meet Bernard. He'd never gone out before. *Why* had she been so stupid as to put the idea in his head? If only there were someone—

Suddenly she thought of the schoolteacher, and ran to the phone. Beside it lay Hannah's letter of condolence, with the printed phone number she had dialled—was it really only last evening? But this time the ringing went unanswered. Mademoiselle would be at her school, and Cécile hadn't that number.

She found she was whimpering to herself, and consciously tightened her control. Mr. Webb? But he was back in Shillingham, and in any case, he did not speak French.

Which left Bernard, who did, and though she was reluctant in the extreme to contact him, at least he could advise her whom to approach.

"Bernard?" As always, she gave the word its French pronunciation. "*C'est moi, Cécile.*" Quickly, she recounted her worries, that Gaston had become lost, or confused, or ill. Worse than that, the fear that stalked her with hooked claws, she refused to acknowledge. She finished her rapid account and waited, breathless, for his response. It didn't come.

"Bernard?" Her voice rose hysterically. "*Au nom de Dieu, aide-moi, je te supplis!*"

"*Mon ange,*" he said, and his voice seemed to throb along the line.

"Tell me what to do!" she implored him. "How many hospitals are there? How can I contact them?"

"Sweetheart, stop worrying. All will be well."

"How *many—*"

"*Cécile, je t'adore.*"

Maddened with frustration, she slammed the phone down and remained for a moment arched over it, her body a curve of despair. The police, then. She'd passed their station on one of her walks about town. Selecting a different pair of shoes, she set off once more, and with increasing hopelessness, on her search. Where could she have gone, a young girl like that?

Cécile halted abruptly, her heart drumming under her ribs. What was she *thinking?* Her acute anxiety had transported her back to her earlier fears for Arlette. But Arlette was dead, and would never come home again. And Gaston? Holy Mother, spare me that.

The police station was further away than she remembered. Or perhaps it was simply that in her frantic haste to get there, the streets seemed unending, as in a dream, when you hurry but cannot move forward. By the time she reached it, her clean blouse was dark with sweat, her shoes pinching as badly as the last pair. Close to exhaustion, she leant on the desk and poured forth a torrent of French, which brought two men forward, to stare at her helplessly. She checked herself, wearily trying to remember such English as she knew. Was this a nightmare? Would she wake to find Gaston sleeping peacefully at her side?

They were kind, these English *flics.* Surprisingly, they already knew he was missing, but, like Bernard, advised her to keep calm. They'd checked the hospitals, and there was no report of his being admitted. That was good news, wasn't it? they said encouragingly.

But was it? What if he lay beneath the dark water, as yet undiscovered?

"And we've men out on the beat, ma'am." (She had no idea what that meant. *Battre?* There was corporal punishment, here in England?) "They've been asked to keep an eye open. He'll turn up safe and sound, you wait and see."

"But he would not—" She broke off helplessly, unable to explain herself in this hateful language.

"There's a foreign film showing at the Regal," one of the men volunteered. "Perhaps he's popped in there."

She didn't believe it, but it was one of a dwindling bundle of straws for her to clutch at. Defeated, she nodded and, with an attempt at a smile, made her endless way back to the hotel.

"David, is that you?"

"Hannah!" Her name was startled out of him, and he was aware of Alan's interest. But she never phoned him at the station—it must be an emergency.

"I've just had a call from Madame Picard. She's out of her mind with worry; apparently her husband left the hotel when she was out this morning, and hasn't been seen since."

Webb's eyes found the clock on the wall. Five o'clock. When Chris phoned back to say Warwick was safely home and had seemingly not left it that day, he'd forced himself to let go and turn his mind to the other matters clamouring for his attention. Now, all his half-formed fears rushed back. "What did you tell her?"

"I promised I'd go straight over. There's no one she can talk to, and she's on the verge of collapse."

"I'll come with you."

"That's what I hoped you'd say. Shall I come down?"

"It would save a detour if you could. Park at the rear of the building. I'll meet you there in five minutes."

"What the hell's happening?" Alan Crombie asked plaintively as Webb dropped the phone.

"I'm going to find out. But it looks as though we might have another body on our hands, and another French one, at that." And without further explanation he strode from the room.

Ten minutes later he was grimly fighting his way through the rush-hour traffic, Hannah, tense, beside him.

"I'd just got back from school," she was saying. "She tried to get me earlier."

"Did she mention Warwick?"

"Only to say he'd not been much help."

"So she must have phoned him. That shows how desperate she is."

"What can have *happened*, David? Surely he wouldn't go off without telling her? It's the first time he's even left his room since they arrived."

"How was he when she left him; did she say?"

"A little better. He was dressed, which he apparently hadn't been for several days. She suggested he might like a breath of air."

"Then panics when he takes her up on it."

"But that was six hours ago!"

"Let's recap. He's under par after the migraines or whatever, and he's still deeply shocked by his daughter's death."

Hannah caught her breath. "You don't think he'd kill himself?"

"I don't think he'd set out to, though he might yield to sudden temptation. Just slide into the river, for instance."

"Surely he'd have more regard for his wife?"

"Hannah, love, if he did do it, he wouldn't have been thinking straight."

"If he did do it," she repeated grimly, "it would fit in very nicely with friend Warwick's plans. Last obstacle removed."

"Exactly, which is why I put the guard on him—or tried to. When I heard he was missing, I immediately checked on Warwick, but he was safely at home and had apparently been there all day. However, if, despite appearances, he somehow managed to winkle Picard out of his room while his wife was out—"

Hannah turned her wide gaze on him. "Go on."

"Let's look at it from Warwick's angle. Any minute now they're going back to France. He still believes the woman'll marry him—or so he says—but suppose he decides to check that Picard'll agree to a divorce. And finds out not only that he knows nothing about it, but that he's no intention of giving up his wife. What then?"

Hannah moistened her lips. "But you said Warwick hadn't been out today."

"I said 'apparently.' We've only his word for it." They were beyond the last, straggling suburbs now, and speeding towards Marlton. "Suppose, just for the sake of argument, that he somehow managed to get Picard into his car. What would he do with him?"

"Talk," Hannah said slowly. "Argue. Try to convince him he'd a prior claim."

"And where would this talk be taking place?"

"Well, he couldn't risk staying in town. Someone might see him. So I suppose he'd drive out—" She stopped. "Oh God, not again!"

"Into the country," Webb finished for her. "And what better place to twist the knife than the spot where the girl died? Softening up the opposition, as it were."

"And you think that, in despair, Picard might have hurled himself after her?"

"That could have been the idea. If he didn't do it voluntarily, he could have been persuaded." Webb paused. "Hang on, we're racing ahead of ourselves. There are several holes in that theory. How did he meet Picard? While he was taking a stroll? Too risky, and too public.

"DI Ledbetter assures me Warwick wasn't spotted at the hotel, and couldn't have got to Picard's room unnoticed. But then the face he was using didn't see Picard leave, so I don't place much reliance on that."

"Perhaps he went out the back way," Hannah said. "That's the quickest route to the carpark."

"Surely to God they'd have covered that. If they didn't, there'll be some rapped knuckles around. To be fair, though, Ledbetter was only humouring me; as far as he's concerned, the case is over. To rethink, then: Warwick couldn't know of the lobby plant, but he'd be manic about secrecy, particularly if he'd foul play in mind. So, if he *did* contact Picard—and remember this is only a hypothesis—he would have told him to use the back entrance."

He slowed down to pass a flock of sheep in the middle of the road. "And if SB left the back of the building unguarded, they probably didn't check on phone calls, either. So we must now find out if Picard received one. There's a call box coming up on the left. You don't know the number of the hotel, by any chance?"

"I'm afraid not."

"Never mind, I'll get it." He swerved into the kerb, drawing up outside the red box. "Won't be a minute." Half way out of the car, he turned back and implanted a hard kiss on her mouth. Her body responded, but her mind was with Madame.

Seconds later, it seemed, David was back beside her and the car was getting up speed again. "Right on the nail," he told her. "A call was put through to the room soon after Madame left this morning. A man's voice, no name asked for or given."

"Did you speak to her?"

"No. No point in adding to her worries at this stage. There'll be time enough to contact her if we're right."

"If we do—find him there, it'll be hard to know if it was murder, accident, or suicide."

"His daughter's case all over again. Except that this time there would be deliberate intent. At best, someone drove him knowingly to the place of her death, and left him there. *If* they did."

Steeple Bayliss High Street was still busy when they reached it, and they had to curb their impatience, crawling behind buses and home-going traffic. Even on Gloucester Road it was slow going, and it was only when Webb turned off on the now-familiar track that he was able to go more quickly. The car bucketed over the uneven ground, rattling and bouncing, and when he stopped it, the sudden silence pressed painfully on their eardrums.

"Stay here," Webb commanded.

"Sorry, I'm coming with you."

He didn't stop to argue, but set off up the slope at a run, holding a hand out behind him. Hannah caught it and ran with him, praying in short, breathless gasps that they wouldn't find what she was so sure would be lying there. When they reached the top, she hung back as David looked over the edge, gripping his fingers tightly.

"He's there," he said. "I'm going down." For the second time in five days, he lowered himself gingerly over the side. Hannah stood where he had left her, eyes stinging with tears. Oh God, how could she face Madame?

"Hannah!" The voice from below had an urgent ring to it. She moved to the edge.

"Yes?"

"I think I heard a groan. We might be in time after all."

"Cécile?"

"Oh, Bernard! I'm insane with worry!"

"You've still heard nothing?"

"*Rien.* He hasn't been taken to hospital, that's all I know."

"Darling, I think you should come here."

"I cannot leave the hotel. There may be news, and also a lady is coming to see me."

"I have the news you're waiting for."

She went still. "About Gaston? You know where he is?"

"I think you should come," he repeated. "There'll be taxis outside the hotel. 14, Lime Tree Grove."

He was waiting on the pavement, helped her out of the car, and paid the driver. Then, with his arm round her, he led her into the house. This was the first of many times, he told himself exultantly, that they'd walk together up this path. After all these years, she belonged to him.

She twisted free of him. "What have you to tell me? Hurry, please, I must not be long. Already there may be messages."

"Come to the kitchen, I've made some coffee."

Impatiently she followed him. The remains of his lunch were still on the table. "I've no time for coffee. Tell me what—"

"There won't be any messages, my darling."

She stared at him while the kitchen clock broke up the stretching seconds into staccato sound, loud as pebbles on a drum. He added gently, "You won't hear from Gaston ever again."

She whispered, white-lipped, "You know where he is?"

"Yes. I should have told you before, but the timing had to be right."

"Where is he? Is he safe? *Tell* me, for God's sake!"

"He's at peace," Bernard said.

"No!" The word was a wail, both hands flying to her head.

"Darling, hush. I mean it. He was tormented, beside himself with grief. I thought it would comfort him to see where she died. Truly, Cécile, I meant it for the best. But he broke away and before I could stop him, he'd leapt over the edge. It took me completely by surprise."

"No, no, no!"

"I know it's hard to bear, my love, but I'm here. We'll see it through together."

"It *can't* be true! Gaston would not kill himself, whatever the pain. It is a mortal sin, Bernard—against his faith. He would suffer any pain rather than that."

"Sweetheart, he was distraught, a desperate, unhappy man. And when I told him of our plans—"

He saw the first doubt in her eyes. "You told him those lies, about my leaving him?" Might that, after all, push him literally over the edge? But no. Gaston's faith would withstand even that. In any case, he wouldn't believe it.

"You must be brave, dearest. It was for the best. His pain is behind him now."

She gazed at him, and her huge eyes seemed to grow even larger. "You're telling me my husband is dead?"

"Darling—"

"Is that what you're telling me?"

"Yes," he said gently. "At peace."

Her breast was heaving, each breath a rasping gasp like a person drowning. She said with difficulty, "I—do not—believe—"

"But you must, sweetheart. Try to accept—"

"—that he would—kill himself," she went on, as though he hadn't spoken. "If he is dead, then—it was you who killed him."

He hesitated, searching the stretched white mask for the features he'd loved so long.

"It was a mercy killing, Cécile. Ending his misery."

"You killed him. You killed my husband. My love."

"Your husband, but not your love. We know better, don't we? Dearest, the shock will pass, then we'll be happy the rest of our lives. The serpents won't trouble us again."

She hadn't heard him. "You killed my love."

He frowned, interpreting it this time not as referring to Gaston, but her love for him. She couldn't mean that after all this time, just when they were free—

He moved impulsively towards her, but she recoiled. "Do not touch me!"

"Beloved—" He reached out to her, but she moved more swiftly. Her hand snaked towards the breadknife lying on the table. Instinctively he crossed his arms over his chest, and gazed in frozen horror as the blade, blinding in a shaft of evening sunlight, swerved instead to his unprotected throat.

Claire had seen the taxi drawing away as she returned from Melbray. Had Beryl come back, or was someone else visiting Bernard? Surely not the Frenchwoman? Though if it were she, then perhaps poor, doubted Bernard had been speaking the truth after all. One way or another, she had to know who the visitor was.

Repeating Simon's ploy of the morning, she caught up a bag of apples—an unlikely gift, but all that was to hand—and hurried to the house next door. The front door was ajar. She tapped with the knocker, and pushed it open. "Bernard? Are you there?"

There was no reply. A profound silence flowed along the hall towards her, a silence which raised the hairs on the back of her neck. She opened her mouth to call again, but instead, obeying she knew not what primeval instinct, went, soft-footed, towards the kitchen. And stood frozen in the doorway.

Bernard lay slumped across the table, his blood gushing in hot, urgent spurts from a gash in his throat. And while she watched, aghast, his eyes glazed over as his life, too, flowed away. Above him, immobile, a knife held in both hands, stood a wild-eyed figure who could only be Cécile Picard. The knife with which Beryl had symbolically stabbed the loaf had found its true target.

Becoming aware of her presence, the woman raised haunted eyes to Claire's. Then she dropped the knife with a clatter and hurled herself into Claire's arms, knocking the bag out of her hand and sending the rosy, shining apples skittering across the floor into the steadily growing pool of blood.

"They'll bring in a verdict of manslaughter," Webb said, his hand stroking Hannah's bare shoulder. "Diminished responsibility. She'll get probation or conditional discharge."

"So she can go back to France?"

"God, yes. The eldest son's flying over to meet them."

"And Monsieur? He's making good progress?"

"Yep. Just as well we found him when we did. In his weakened state, he mightn't have lasted the night."

Hannah said slowly, "It's ironic, isn't it, that a strong and healthy girl broke her neck when she fell accidentally, while her father, older and considerably more feeble, survived a deliberate push."

"But what Warwick hadn't realised was that Arlette's death was due to two factors. First, she had exceptionally brittle bones, which she obviously didn't inherit from her father. And second, it was the angle at which she fell which proved fatal. There was no guarantee that someone else, falling from virtually the same place, would also be killed. In fact, if Picard had been a stronger man, he could well have picked himself up and climbed back up the hillside. As it was, he twisted his ankle and, of course, was in a weak condition to start with."

"And the other irony is that, since her husband wasn't dead after all, Madame needn't have killed the professor."

"Ah, but that was fate, wasn't it? The tragic outcome demanded by melodrama. The classics are full of these heroic figures, who consider the world well lost for love. You seldom come across them in real life, but Bernard Warwick was a prime example. La Picard was like a drug to him, and he'd suffered withdrawal symptoms for thirty years. No wonder his mind snapped when he found her again. People thought him cold and self-contained, yet he was capable of such a deep and lasting passion that it warped his whole personality. Not many of us could cope with a love like that."

He turned his head towards her, and his tone lightened. "Mind you, I'm willing to have a go, if you are. How about it? Care to try your hand at some deep and lasting passion?"

Hannah propped herself on one elbow, looking down into his smiling face. Gently, she traced the outline of his mouth with one finger.

"You might just have talked me into it," she said.

About the Author

Anthea Fraser, who lives in England, has published numerous novels and short stories both here and abroad; her work has been translated into seven languages. DEATH SPEAKS SOFTLY is her third novel for the Crime Club. Her previous Crime Club titles are *A Shroud for Delilah* and *Pretty Maids All in a Row.*